BETTER FRAMES
FOR YOUR PICTURES

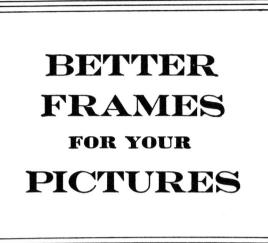

BETTER FRAMES
FOR YOUR
PICTURES

by

FREDERIC TAUBES

A Studio Book

THE VIKING PRESS • NEW YORK

Distributed in Canada by
The Macmillan Company of Canada Limited

SBN 670-15991-3 (hardbound)
    670-02006-0 (paperback)

Library of Congress catalog card number: 68-22318

Printed in U.S.A.

ACKNOWLEDGMENTS

To my assistant and associate, Donald Pierce, I wish to
express thanks for collaboration on finishing many frames
reproduced in this book. My thanks are also due to William
Zeller of Nanuet, New York, for photographing all the
frames finished by Mr. Pierce and myself; and to Lewensohn
Co., Inc., and F.A.R. Gallery for furnishing photographs
of their own frames.

CONTENTS

Finishes). Solid-Gold Finish with Metal Leaves. Comparison of the Different Metal Leaves Available. Step-by-Step Procedure in Applying Metal Leaf on the Primed Surface of a Frame. (Variation *A* for Metal Leaf with Antique Effect. Variation *B* for Gold with Antique Effect. Ornaments in Gold and Silver Leaf. Glazing and Tarnishing Metal-Leaf Surfaces.) General Notes on Gilding.

PREFACE

In the preface to the first edition I stated that the aim of this book was to show the reader how to finish or make his own frames by very simple means. I also mentioned that only painters with a lucrative trade—an infinitesimal number of people —could afford to buy really good frames. Such frames are not available in every community—and this is another reason why the majority of artists are compelled to use standard moldings obtainable in lumber yards, or to buy raw-wood moldings from artists' supply stores and finish these themselves.

I also stressed the need of choosing or making a frame that was in character with the painting it was to enclose. Just as an appropriate frame enhances the beauty of a painting, a poorly chosen one can greatly detract from it. Every picture looks twice as important if it is framed with taste and imagination.

A NOTE ABOUT NEW PREPARATIONS

The basic principles of frame-making have not changed since this book was first published, but the means of accomplishing certain objectives have undergone some important modifications as new materials have been developed. These have considerably simplified some procedures.

For example, there are relatively new acrylic materials: colors, medium, gesso, and modeling paste. These are all water-based and become water-insoluble when dry. They allow colors to be superimposed almost immediately without isolating the successive applications of glazes or solid, opaque colors. Consequently, the acrylic medium is more practical than glue size as a binder for dry pigments.

On many occasions acrylic gesso is preferable to traditional gesso. It dries faster and is more opaque. The advantage of acrylic modeling paste is that it comes ready-prepared, thus obviating the necessity of compounding a thick glue-based gesso. The handling of these acrylic products is described on page 32.

The amateur can avoid the rather difficult process of gold-leafing using the traditional water-gilding method if he avails himself of certain materials discussed on page 101.

The instructions for handling these new preparations are the only important techniques that need to be added to this edition; traditional processes described earlier remain the same.

New York, 1968

1

THE AVAILABILITY OF FRAMES AND
THEIR RELATIVE COST

As I have stated, one cannot count on having frames made to order in small communities. Furthermore, buying frames from a catalogue is always precarious, for, even assuming that the finish is in good taste, the particular frame still may not prove satisfactory for the painting the purchaser has in mind. The molding may be too heavy or light, or the shape, or the color may be wrong. It stands to reason that if a frame is finished at home for a specific picture, the harmony between frame and picture can more readily be established.

Let us consider for a moment the cost of frames. This is an item with which practically all painters are greatly concerned, for it is a constantly recurring expense. To those who only occasionally have a painting or a print to frame, it is a less pressing question. With the exception of the raw-wood frame, every fine, well-finished frame is quite costly and the hand-carved ones are fabulous. It may often seem unreasonable that a relatively simple gesso-finished[1] frame of small size (about 16″ x 20″) costs anywhere from ten dollars up and is often more than twice that price. It would seem that perhaps the manufacturers of frames or the picture shops have embarked upon a get-rich-quick scheme; but this, as I well know, is not the case. Here is the rather simple arithmetic: It takes from two to perhaps six hours (on an elaborate molding) to finish a frame properly in gesso and gold. And as frame finishing and gilding are skilled labor, the cost of even a modest frame must, therefore, be high. On the other hand, an already made up medium size, raw-wood frame will cost around $2.50, and the finish of it, when worked on at home, will add only a few more pennies to the total cost. Or you may be able to pick up an old frame at an auction or

---

[1] One of the most popular frame finishes today, described later in the book.

an antique dealers for a nominal sum and refinish it at home for equally little.

THE GENERAL CHARACTER OF FRAMES

Frames that are commonly used today fall into four distinct categories: (1) Raw-wood frames, these rely chiefly or entirely on the effect produced by the nature of the wood grain (figs. 2, 3, 4, 8, 9, 10). (2) Frames finished in simple gesso, plain or patterned (figs. 14, 15, 17, 18). (3) Frames finished in gesso with additional carving and gilding (figs. 12 and 26-31). (4) Carved (or composition) facsimiles of "period" frames, such as the Barbizon or Baroque types, and the like (figs. 34 and 35).

We may as well face the fact that those in the last category that may be required for formal portraits, or an "old master," perhaps, cannot be produced by an amateur frame maker. In any case these Barbizon frames (unless carved in wood) are finished in a composition compound too fragile to stand the rough handling and shipping such as is accorded to them at exhibitions or in art galleries. Painters have found that when their paintings have been around to exhibitions for a while, the more fragile frames are ready for the scrap heap. However, the Barbizon patterns are made also in papier-mâché. This material has the advantage of extra-light weight and a fair durability (fig. 35).

Lastly, there are a great variety of commercial moldings (old and relatively new) which can be found at sundry out-of-the-way stores, at auctions, and junk shops—even in your attic. Although these frames are often in poor taste according to contemporary standards, there are exceptions which always make a search worth while. These frames will usually require fixing up and refinishing (see chapter VIII). An ordinary hard-looking frame in solid gold finish can be quite transformed by painting it in gesso or else by antiquing it as described in chapter VII.

THE APPEARANCE OF THE FRAME FINISH

That the style of painting is strongly influenced by fashions cannot be denied. The same goes for frames too, although here the change is not as rapid. As a characteristic phenomenon in complete change of taste, we have the present fashion for worm-eaten and weather-beaten frames which, a generation ago, would have been totally unacceptable. However, frame makers do not compete with painters in the speed of changing their styles every season.

Taking it all in all, we may say that too much ornamentation, too much gilt, the newness and perfection of the finish have been out of style for a generation or so. Although a lot of gilding, even if applied with machine-made precision, need not necessarily be called vulgar, the sheen natural to a solid surface of gold may become disturbing inasmuch as it can detract from the "sheen"—metaphorically speaking—which belongs to the painting proper. Altogether a look of shiny newness combined with mechanically perfect finish, as well as excessive gloss and overornamentation, should be avoided in any frame.

The ideal finish for most frames is gesso, described in chapter IV. Natural wood is also very desirable in many instances; but, as we shall see a little later, only a few kinds of wood are suitable for use in unfinished condition.

The color of frames used for an oil painting should, as a rule, be neutral, that is, of a gray tonality. This tonality can be modified by brownish, reddish, bluish, or yellowish hues, depending upon which is in greatest harmony with the predominating color of the picture. And where the picture has found a definite home, the color of the walls and the room furnishings in which it is housed should also be considered. From this we see the great practicality of the neutral-colored frame which does not clash either with the picture or the colors of the room whatever they may be.

Narrow profiles, carvings, and some particular sections of the molding can be gilded with good effect. However, unless a picture is to be used in a definite "period room," these surfaces should rarely, if ever, be solidly gilded for the reasons already described. For the fashionable "antique" appearance, only traces of gold should remain, so the frame will look as though time had left its mark on it. How this can be successfully accomplished is described in chapter VII.

Some of the most sought after frames today are simple wood frames that appear as if they had endured much hardship. This "driftwood look" is designed to enchant us (as it undoubtedly does), whereas our grandfathers delighted in "overstuffed," heavily gilded gingerbread monstrosities that have long since gone out of fashion. Undoubtedly, we have come to look upon the older, more primitive antiques (the good ones, anyway) as things of beauty. This simplicity is, at it seems, more in keeping with our present-day manner of living.

For water colors, pastels, and most types of graphic work, the finish of the frame, because of the delicacy of these media (as compared with the more robust appearance of oil paint) should, generally speaking, be even less pronounced in color. A light gesso wash on a coarse-grained hard wood is especially suitable (see fig. 8).

For black and white or sepia lithographs and etchings, I prefer using simple oak or wormy chestnut moldings unfinished or carrying faint traces of a patina, as illustrated by diagram IV.

You will find the subject of framing water colors, pastels, prints, etc. taken up in more detail in chapter VI.

DESIGNS FOR MOLDINGS

Not only the finish but the design of the molding as well will influence the appearance and beauty of a frame to a great extent. Moreover, the design of the molding—that is, the arrangement of profiles (see diagram I) or the presence of ornaments and carvings—will dictate which part of the frame should be gilded and which merely gessoed. For example, narrow profiles, narrow flat surfaces between profiles, and delicate ornaments and carvings will be especially suitable for gilding, whereas wide, plain surfaces will look better when treated in gesso.

Moldings can be ordered from a lumber mill after your own design. If you take a drawing of the profile required they will reproduce it. When two hundred feet or more of a design is bought, a mill does not, as a rule, charge for "setting up the knife." If they do, the charge is very small. Of course raw-wood moldings of various designs can also be obtained in foot length

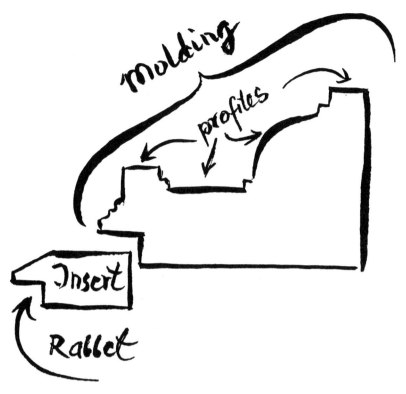

Diagram I. Cross-section of a molding (actual size) and its component parts. The insert is a separate frame which fits onto the rabbet of the frame, and is attached to it by brads.

from some frame dealers or specialized lumber yards, or ready-made raw-wood frames in standard sizes can be bought in art supply stores. For sources of supply, see the end of the book.

Before going into the details of how to make a frame from various moldings, it should be known that these are cut from lumber of standard dimensions such as 1″ x 1″, 1″ x 2″, 2″ x 2″, 2″ x 3″, etc. The size of the lumber, not the design, determines the price.

For those who may not be well acquainted with the different parts that make up a frame, diagrams II, III, and IV should prove to be useful. These cross-sectional diagrams are all reproduced in original size.

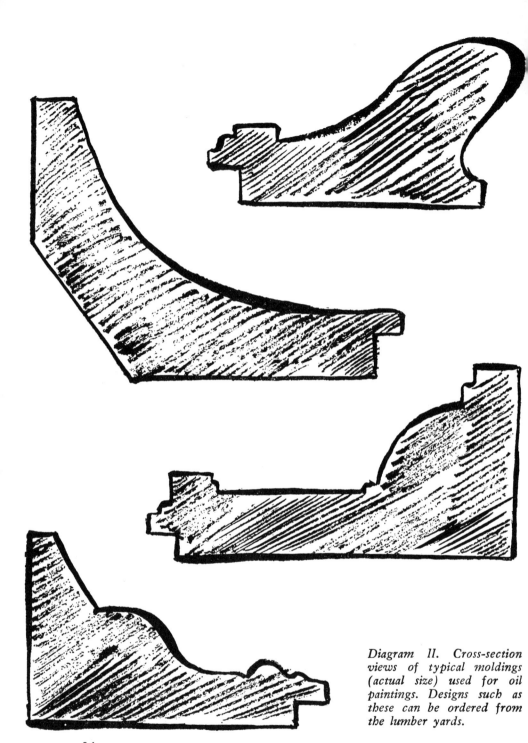

Diagram 11. Cross-section views of typical moldings (actual size) used for oil paintings. Designs such as these can be ordered from the lumber yards.

Diagram II shows moldings of various typical designs used for oil paintings. The profile can be varied to suit any particular taste, but I would not advocate any radical departure from these well-thought-out designs.

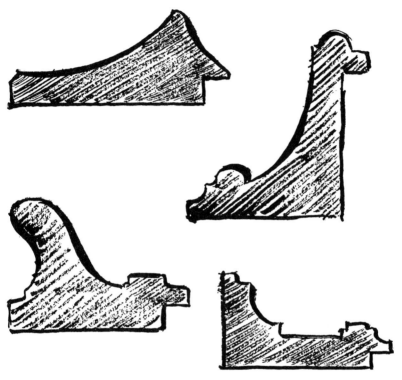

Diagram III. Cross-section views of moldings (actual size) suitable for water colors and drawings.

Diagram III shows suggested moldings for water colors and drawings, while diagram IV represents those suitable for prints, lithographs, etchings, etc. Frames suitable for reproductions you will find illustrated in chapter X.

When you are buying ready-made moldings or made-up raw-wood frames, it would be well to keep in mind the principle designs represented in these diagrams.

Diagram IV. Cross-section views of moldings for prints, drawings, etc.

MAKING FRAMES FROM BUILDERS' MOLDINGS

Standard builders' moldings such as are commonly available in most lumber yards can very well be utilized in making frames. These moldings are used by carpenters for various interior finishing, such as door or window frames. They are quite inexpensive. As a rule, several types will have to be combined to produce an effective frame for an oil painting. Two, three, or even more molding strips will be assembled, the widest molding forming the base for the others (see diagram IX).

Ordinary stock-size lumber can be used as the base of the frame on which the builders' moldings are joined. However, in some instances, according to the effect desired and the type and size of molding chosen, one single molding may serve (see diagrams IV and V).

Should you desire to carve any of these simple builders' moldings into some surface design for a frame, you can get satisfactory results by using a gouge or rasp. A few carvings that are very easy to make are given in chapter VIII.

The next thing to consider when purchasing builders' molding is that, unlike ready-made raw-wood frame molding, it has no rabbet. The rabbet is, of course, required to hold the canvas stretchers of an oil painting, as shown in diagram I, or to hold the glass and the mount of a water color.

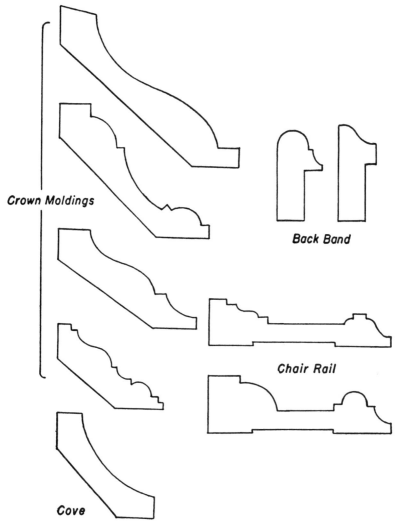

Crown Moldings

Back Band

Chair Rail

Cove

Diagrams V and VI. Different type builders' moldings for use in the construction of frames.

If one is lucky enough to have access to an electric bench saw, a groove for the rabbet can be made quickly and easily, assuming that the design of the molding will allow it. This must be done before the moldings are assembled into a frame. Another way of making a rabbet for an oil painting frame, regardless of the design of the molding, is to glue or nail small strips of wood about ½″ square to the back of the molding, ⅜″ away from the inside (see diagrams VII to X). The proper time to do this is after the frame has been joined. (For mitering and joining frames, see chapter IX).

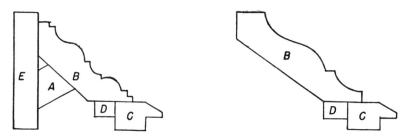

Diagrams VII and VIII. Combinations of builders' moldings. (A) Wedge supporting the crown molding. (B) Crown molding. (C) Insert. (D) Strip of wood added to molding to form the rabbet on molding (B). (E) Baseboard.

In diagrams V to XII a few of the many sizes and designs of builders' moldings are represented. Since the insert (see chapter V) is now almost a required part of modern framing, it has been included in all the combinations illustrated. It is not essential to have it, but it always sets a painting off well. A molding 1″ to 1¼″ wide and ½″ thick which can be used for an insert is generally found in lumber yards. All one has to do is to make a rabbet by one or the other methods explained in the preceding paragraph.

By experimenting with various types of moldings, many pleasing combinations can be worked out. The actual cutting and joining of separate pieces is described in chapter IX. Here are a few suggestions for assembling builders' moldings:

Diagram VII. This represents the simplest type of frame. It consists of a crown molding with an insert. The top outside edge can be finished like the rest of the molding in gesso, or it can receive some ornamentation, and gilding.

Diagram VIII. This frame is made of a crown molding and a ½″ x 2½″ flat outside-edge piece. First, the molding is mitered and assembled (see chapter IX). Then the outside edge piece is cut and assembled to fit the molding. The two pieces should be glued, then nailed together with brads of suitable length before the glue is set. The frame is given further support by the insertion in the back of several small wedge-shaped blocks which should be fastened on with glue (marked *A* on diagram VIII). Lastly, the strips to form the rabbet to hold the insert are added.

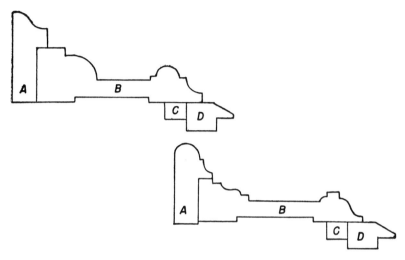

Diagrams IX and X. Combinations of builders' moldings. (A) Backband. (B) Chair-rail molding. (C) Strips to form rabbet. (D) Insert.

Diagrams IX and X. These two frames are constructed in the same manner as the above, the only difference being in the design of the profiles which in both instances are chair-rail moldings. A piece of backband (diagram VI) is added to raise the height of the outside edge. Because the backband carries a rabbet, it is best to assemble the molding first, cut and assemble the backband to fit, then fasten molding and backband together with glue and brads. Finally the strips are added to the back to form a rabbet in the same way as described earlier.

Diagram XI. A flat strip of board (base piece) ¾″ x 2½″, an outside edge piece ½″ x 3″, a piece of cove molding (diagram V), and a piece of backband are the components of this frame. The four pieces are glued and nailed together as shown (nail before the glue has set), then mitered. Before mitering, however, it is important to predetermine where the cuts will be made, so that the nails will not fall in line with the saw blade. In this frame, the rabbet of the backband holds the insert, which also has a rabbet to hold the canvas stretcher.

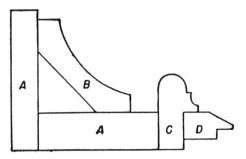

Diagram XI. Combinations of builders' moldings. (A) Baseboard. (B) Cove molding. (C) Backband. (D) Insert.

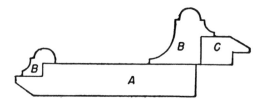

Diagram XII. Combinations of builders' moldings. (A) Baseboard. (B) Picture-frame molding. (C) Insert.

Diagram XII. This frame is composed of a stock-size flat base piece ¾" x 4" and two pieces of small picture-frame molding. The larger of these picture-frame moldings on the inside edge of the frame is cut and joined first. After the large flat piece has been rabbeted on the outside edge, and the small molding set in with glue and brads, it is mitered and assembled to fit the flat molding. The back outside edge of the base is beveled off with a plane. The rabbet referred to on the top outside of the flat piece can be produced with a power bench saw or else this should be done at the mill of the lumber yard.

RELATION OF THE PAINTING TO THE DIMENSIONS AND TYPE OF FRAME

Oil paintings from about 10" x 12" to a 30" x 40" size generally look best in a frame 4" wide. Those over 30" x 40" may look better with a 6" or even an 8" molding. However, as the larger frames are quite expensive, you can often manage well enough by using a 4" frame and an insert of from 1" to 2". These examples represent ideal proportions, but often painters use a 4" frame for the largest as well as the smallest pictures, and sometimes even narrower moldings for the sake of economy.

Occasionally you see a large painting with a 1" or 1½" molding, but this ceases to represent a "frame" in the true sense—it simply boxes in the stretchers. This may be acceptable for exhibition purposes if you haven't a larger molding, or for shipping purposes. Moldings of ½" are sometimes used as a protective lattice nailed onto the sides of the stretcher bars to protect the canvas while in storage or in transit.

The depth of the molding should also be well considered. A 2½" depth is best for all moldings. Even in a small frame this depth is not excessive, provided that the frame has an insert (see diagram I and VIII). Frames of less than 1½" depth should never be used for oil paintings. The surface of a frame which is almost flush with the surface of a painting is always unattractive.

Diagram XIII. Two characteristic styles of inserts (actual size): (left) with short bevel, (right) with extended bevel.

As the framing of water colors, prints, etc. follows a different principle, the question of suitable moldings for this type of work is taken up later. See chapter VI.

Choice of a Molding for Different Style Pictures

We established in the preface that the color or character of a particular frame finish will enhance or disturb the general effect of a painting; also that the type of the ornaments and the carving will contribute in large measure to the total effect. It is not possible to establish a hard and fast rule whereby a certain type of painting should have a certain type of frame or ornamentation. However, the following principle will guide us in the right direction when selecting frames. Paintings that show many intricate details or small or detached brush strokes will look best in frames that carry little ornamentation and are finished in subdued colors. Conversely, a painting showing large, quiet surfaces can offset a more lively frame, that is, one having more carvings, gilding, and stronger emphasis on textural effects.

INSERTS AND MATS AS PART OF THE FRAME

We must remember that, in framing oil paintings, the width of the frame will be enlarged and its depth increased when an insert is used. As a rule, inserts should be 1″ to 1¼″ wide, of which about ¼″ will be hidden by the rabbet (diagram I). Even in the smallest oil paintings a total width of 1″ for this insert should be maintained. On large paintings 1¼″ to 1½″ is a good average, though occasionally you can make it as large as 2″ if the frame is rather narrow for the painting. Sometimes when fitting an oil painting to an existing frame, the insert can help make up a slight difference in size.

The use of inserts as developed in chapter V is something of an innovation. The purpose is to create an intermediate surface, like a mat, between an oil painting and the frame. A narrow insert covered with raw painter's linen (burlap is too coarse a material for an elegant effect) looks especially well mediating, as it were, between the painting and the frame (figs. 2, 3, and 4). The insert can also be finished in a neutral gray gesso applied directly to the wood (see figs. 9, 11, and 12). You can also use any other subdued tone that harmonizes with the total effect of the painting and the chosen color of the frame. For small oil paintings, especially, an insert is almost indispensable, for it gives the painting more breathing space. However, a simple scoop design such as seen in diagram I (top left) does not require an insert, for the gently curved quiet surface of the frame makes an insert superfluous.

The difference between an insert and a mat is that the former is made from flat surfaced wood molding about 1″ to 2″ wide, with a rabbet cut in the back (upon which the stretcher of the oil painting rests), whereas a mat is generally made of white or colored cardboard and should be at least 2½″ wide even for the smallest water color, drawing, or print. Mats often carry a simple design such as seen in fig. 24. Besides thin cardboard mats, there are also those made of fiberboard of various thicknesses. The thickness allows treating the beveled edge in a special fashion as described in chapter VI and illustrated in fig. 25.

To summarize then, most oil paintings look better with an insert, although this is not absolutely essential. Water colors and prints should be framed in a mat which serves the same purpose as an insert. Instructions on the making and finishing of inserts are given in chapter V; on mats in chapter VI.

2

MATERIALS FOR FINISHING FRAMES

(Sources of supply are given at the end of the book.)

You will not need all the following items for finishing or refinishing a frame because naturally some will be used for one type of finish and others for another. However, it is better to list all the materials together here and give a brief description of each so you may become familiar with them. The materials needed for any one type of finish are listed at the head of the step-by-step instructions for that finish in other chapters.

Whiting. This is a white pigment (powdered chalk) sold by weight and used in the preparation of gesso, described later in the present chapter.

Casein, hide glue, or gelatin. (These are needed for the preparation of gesso, also for patina, and glue color described shortly.) Casein comes in powder form, ready to be mixed with hot water. Glue is sold in sheets, flakes, or granules. To make a proper solution, you should soak it overnight in water before you heat it to complete the solution. Gelatin (any form of it, technical grade or such as is used for cooking) dissolves readily in hot water.

Copal Varnish. This comes in many brands. The product manufactured by Permanent Pigments of Cincinnati, Ohio, which is compounded after my formula, is especially adapted for preparation of the varnish color (the alternative to using glue color), and for the making of carnauba wax paste for gilding (chapter VII).

Dry pigments. Black, ultramarine blue, iron oxide red, umber, burnt sienna, yellow ocher will take care of just about all requirements. One need not buy the expensive artists' pigments for frame finishes. The materials sold by weight in hardware and paint stores are good enough for our purposes; they are cheap and should be bought in one-pound quantities. These are to be used for coloring gesso, patina, glue color or varnish color, and raw-wood moldings.

Gum resins. For coloring metallic surfaces we shall require the gum resins *gamboge* and *dragon's blood.* (See sources of supply at the end of the book.)

India ink. Black and brown India ink are often used for coloring, or rather "antiquing," gesso and metallic surfaces.

Alcohol (ethanol) added to water is needed to dissolve (disperse) ivory-black pigment. Alcohol is also used for dissolving the gum resins and for washing brushes used with shellac.

Shellac (white or orange, in concentration such as sold in paint stores) is used for making varnish color as well as glue color water resistant to subsequent aqueous applications such as gesso. It is also used for making the red priming foundation for metallic applications nonabsorbent, and for dissolving gum resins. *Orange shellac* will deepen the color of gold and make silver leaf appear like light gold. *White shellac* should be used fresh, for when old and oxidized, shellac dries poorly and remains sticky.

Turpentine is necessary in the preparation of carnauba wax paste (chapter VII).

Carnauba wax, obtained from leaves of certain Brazilian palm trees, is the only product which can be satisfactorily used for wax gilt (chapter VII). It is also excellent for general waxing.

Bronze powder (in the lightest color obtainable). *Gold or imitation gold leaf. Silver or aluminum leaf.* Any one of these can be used for the gilding process. The powders are sold in bottles (or vials) and the leaf in book form (chapter VII).

Japan size or, still better, *synthetic gold size* (which dries more quickly than the former) will be used as a mordant (adhesive) for the metallic leaf applications (chapter VII).

Sulphur powder, when mixed with water and brushed over silver and aluminum leaf will tarnish the metals and produce an "antique" effect (chapter VII).

Rottenstone is a gray powder used in connection with the antique finish described in finishes 6 and 7 in chapter III.

Wood bleach, a commercial product sold in paint and hardware stores, is used to bleach stained moldings such as mahogany, walnut, oak, when a new lighter natural finish is desired. (In most cases a concentrated solution of Clorox will bleach wood effectively.)

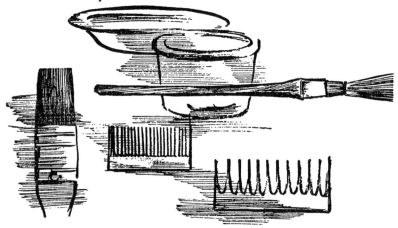

Diagram XIV. Tools for gessoing: bowls, brushes, and combs.

TOOLS FOR FINISHING FRAMES
(fig. 1 and diagram XIV)

Utility brushes (house painter type) will be needed in sizes of ½″ to 2″ for applying gesso, patina, shellac, etc. (N.B. Always keep your brushes clean. Those used for gesso, patina, glue color and varnish color should be washed clean with soap and hot water. Shellac should be washed off with alcohol, and Japan size and the synthetic mordant—used for metal leaf applications—should be washed off with benzine, mineral spirits, or a commercial dry-cleaning fluid.)

Small dishes and one-pint *pans.* You should have a few of these handy for mixing the materials.

Three gouges, ⅛″, ¼″, and ½″ wide, will be needed if you plan to do some carving (chapter VIII).

Round wood rasps (so-called rattail). You may need these in ⅛″, ¼″, and ½″ sizes for carving where a gouge cannot be used (chapter VIII).

A flat wood rasp will be needed for the rounding of sharp frame edges when a softer effect is desired (chapter VIII).

Combs. Ordinary hair combs will be used for making patterns on the gesso (see finishes 12 and 13 in chapter IV).

Modeling tool. (See fig. 1, extreme right.) This will be used for making designs in gesso, as shown in fig. 21.

Knife. This is for cutting mats (see fig. 1, second from left).

Compass, steel ruler, and sometimes a *square* will also be needed in connection with making mats (chapter VIII).

Sandpaper, No. 00, and a *fine steel wool* for polishing. Rougher grades of sandpaper may be needed for smoothing rough wood surfaces and in connection with refinishing of old frames. It is always useful to keep several grades of sandpaper on hand.

If you are going to make your own frames, a list of tools is given in chapter IX.

The above may seem like a formidable list of materials and tools, but as we said earlier, you will need only certain of them unless you attempt all the operations described in the book. They are all of the common type, and quite inexpensive. Moreover, some of the implements, such as brushes, pans, combs, etc., will be found around the house, and some others undoubtedly can be improvised.

PREPARATION OF MATERIALS

Before specific instructions are given for different frame finishes in the following chapters, there are a few processes common to the preparation of materials for most of the finishes. We shall discuss them here to avoid unnecessary repetition later.

In finishing raw-wood frames you will want to know how to prepare a "pickle" which will allow the attractive texture and natural grain of the wood to assert itself (see fig. 7 and others). For this effect, which is currently so much in favor, you will need to use what is called, for convenience, *glue color* or *varnish color.* You can also use a *patina* for a similar effect, as well as for "antiquing" frames that have been treated with gesso or finished in gold.

The formula for gesso will also be required for a great many of the finishes. And let us make clear at this point that gesso, a rather formidable-sounding word to many people, could not be simpler to prepare and it is applied to a frame like any paint. As stated before, the gesso finish is suited in one variation or another to almost any type of oil painting, water color, or reproduction. A number of practical gesso finishes, with step-by-step directions, are given in chapter IV.

Glue Color or *Varnish Color*

This is a thin color finish, one without much body (in contrast to gesso which is heavy bodied and opaque). Glue color or varnish color is frequently used in the finishing of raw-wood frames, permitting the texture of the wood to show through. What the mixture really amounts to is a glue size or varnish with pigment added for coloring.* This material is also sometimes used over a gesso for the effects described under different specific finishes given later in the book.

Glue Color

Glue color is made with any of three different bases: glue, casein, or gelatin.

Select any one of these substances and dissolve one ounce in one pint of water. Of the three alternatives, casein should be the first choice as it does not jell when cool. And casein is more versatile in other ways. Whereas glue and gelatin in a weaker mixture than that indicated above lose their adhesive power, casein will remain effective even if greatly thinned with water. Any of these three glue colors decomposes quickly if it is not kept in a refrigerator. However, the addition of 1 per cent of a 10 per cent phenol solution will preserve them indefinitely in an average temperature, provided that they are kept in well-stoppered bottles. (Phenol, also known as carbolic acid, is an effective germicide obtainable in drugstores.)

These glue colors, or sizes, will serve to bind the pigment. Any pigment can be used according to the color effect desired. The following dry pigments, sold by the pound in hardware or paint stores, will take care of most requirements: umber, yellow

---

* See information about new preparations in the Preface.

ocher, burnt sienna, ultramarine blue, iron oxide red, and ivory black. With the exception of ivory black, any of these pigments can be mixed with the size to the tonality required by means of a brush. The black pigment does not easily mix with size, but this difficulty can be overcome by adding a small amount of alcohol (ethanol or methanol).

Varnish Color

Varnish color can be used instead of glue color in most cases, *except* for the red ground necessary for gilding. Varnish color is easier to prepare than glue size. All that has to be done is to mix a sufficient quantity of dry pigment with varnish until the required coloring is achieved and the consistency is similar to that of a dense water color. The mixing is done with the brush you will use for applying the varnish color to the frame.

Both varnish color and glue color must, upon drying, receive a coat of shellac to prevent their being dissolved by subsequent application of gesso or patina. The actual application of these colors is described in step-by-step instructions under specific frame finishes in the next two chapters.

One can also use standard water-color paints instead of varnish color or glue color, but the expense is far greater.

India Ink

Mention should also be made of India ink, which is an excellent coloring and "antiquing" matter. Being waterproof, it does not require shellac protection to prevent it from dissolving when any subsequent aqueous applications are used *on top* of it. India ink should be used by itself (that is, not mixed with size or any other pigment) and applied in full strength, or just rubbed into the gesso surface or raw-wood molding for a light effect.

Earth Pigments

Earth pigments such as umber, ocher, sienna, etc., can be mixed with water, brushed onto raw-wood moldings, and rubbed with a rag into the fiber of the wood. This will darken the color of the wood but leave the texture of the grain showing.

Gesso

This material, used in past ages for the coating of wood prior to finishing in color or gold, consisted of a white pigment, such as powdered chalk, mixed with a glue size. This formula has not changed from then to our day except that, instead of the natural calcium carbonate, the more opaque form—whiting—is used in combination with titanium white. If one wishes to prepare gesso in the traditional way in the studio, mix two pounds of whiting (or powdered chalk) with one pint of casein size or glue size (made of one pint of water to one ounce of glue or casein). This will produce a thick creamy solution. However, this glue mixture, once the whiting has been added, will have to be kept warm in a double boiler, otherwise it will congeal upon cooling and become unusable.

All things considered, under present conditions there is no reason why a painter should not avail himself of *the more practical modern materials* sold in most paint and hardware stores. First of all there are the ready-mixed dry gesso compounds which need only be dissolved in hot water to a pastelike consistency (see sources of supply at the end of the book). Most of the commercially processed gesso materials are of excellent quality. More practical still I find the casein white paints that sell under such trade names as Kem-Tone, Luminall, etc. These latter paints must be thinned a little with water so they will brush onto the frame easily. Being of a puttylike consistency, they are well adapted for the impression of patterns or designs such as seen in figs. 13 to 21 and others.*

These paints are equally adaptable to the preparation of the patina, described below. Henceforth, when I refer to gesso it will be the preparation made from any of the above ingredients, more particularly to the casein paints which, however, must be used *only* in white for the first coat.

Whichever mixture you use for gessoing, the material should be brought to a thick creamy texture, just thin enough to allow

* See information about new preparations in the Preface.

for easy spreading with a brush on the wood surface without leaving heavy brush marks.

Gray Patina

This material (always mixed to a shade of gray) serves the purpose of antiquing the finish on raw-wood, gesso, or gilded frames. It is prepared from the gesso paste, just described, with enough water added to make it much thinner. It should be about halfway between the thickness of the gesso and the glue color. In other words, it should be just thick enough to preserve opacity. The patina should be colored with a little raw umber pigment to produce a neutral tone. For cooler grays, ultramarine or black can be added to the umber. For a yellowish tone, the umber should be slightly tempered with ocher and for greenish effects black and ocher should be used. Only the colors mentioned are suitable for the patina, for it should always be neutral in character.

Priming for Metallic Applications

A colored base is required whenever the use of gold, silver, or aluminum leaf is contemplated. An iron oxide red pigment or umber (or black for silver or aluminum leaf) bound by a glue size to a fairly thick consistency will produce the foundation for the metals. The preparation and application of this priming is described in more detail in chapter VII.

Wax Paste

The final step in most of the frame finishes described in the following chapter calls for the application of wax. Waxing is *always* the last operation; either beeswax (any good commercial brand will do) or carnauba wax should be used. The formula for the preparation of the beeswax paste is as follows: one part beeswax to three parts turpentine (first by weight, second by volume).

Preparation of the carnauba wax paste is more complicated. How to make it is described at the beginning of chapter VII, where it is needed as the binder for bronze powder in the process of gilding. The advantage of using carnauba wax paste rather than beeswax for polishing the finished frame is that it makes a much harder and more durable finish.

Whichever of the two wax paste preparations you are using, the application is the same. Take a little of the paste up on a rag and spread it over the frame sparingly, polishing it into a gloss just as you would any delicate piece of furniture.

A Word on the Use of Acrylic Materials

As mentioned in the Preface, *acrylic gesso,* once applied, becomes water-insoluble and therefore does not require isolation by the application of shellac or varnish. However, in its original condition it is too thick, retaining undesirable brush marks that cannot be easily sandpapered. Therefore, this gesso should be thinned to the consistency of milk. It will then require at least three separate applications to render it sufficiently opaque.

The *acrylic medium* is a substitute for glue size. It will serve for binding pigments (white or colored) and is water-insoluble when dry. In this new acrylic system the patina (described on page 31) may be prepared by adding any of the desired dry pigments (or ready-prepared acrylic colors) to the thinned acrylic gesso.

Lastly, *acrylic modeling paste* serves for the creation of decorative patterns and sculptured effects (see page 65), as well as for the restoration of ornaments on new and antique frames. The white paste can be mixed with colored pigments, but when it becomes too thick, some of the acrylic medium should be added to it to improve its adhesive properties.

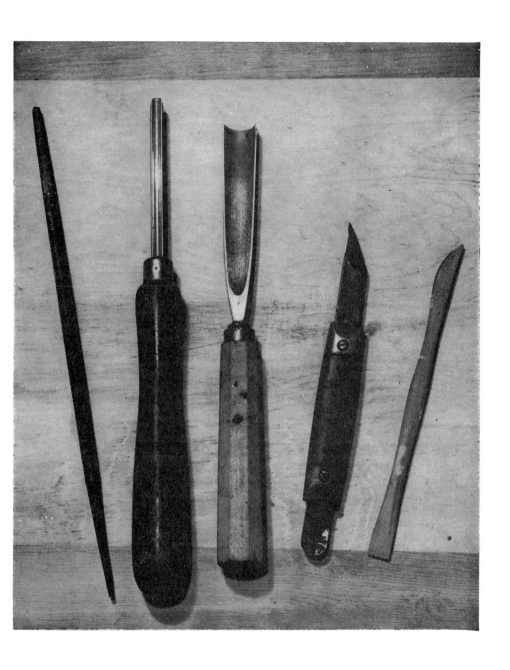

Fig. 1. Tools. Left to right: wood rasp, two gouges, knife for cutting mats, and a molding tool.

Fig. 2 (above). Oak frame covered with umber pigment mixed with water alone, and treated with a light patina. The reproduction, used for demonstration purposes, is a detail from a painting by Peter Brueghel.

Fig. 2A. Corner detail of the frame shown in fig. 2.

34

Fig. 3. Oak molding darkened with umber and ultramarine glue color and treated with a light gray patina.

35

Fig. 4. Raw-wood wormy chestnut molding colored with glue color and treated with a gray patina.

37

Fig. 5 (above). Oak panel scorched by means of a blow torch.

Fig. 6 (right). Covering a scorched oak panel with a thin coat of white gesso.

Fig. 7 (below). The finished "pickled" effect of the oak panel after steps shown in figs. 5 and 6 and after rubbing off excess gesso, leaving it in the crevices of the wood.

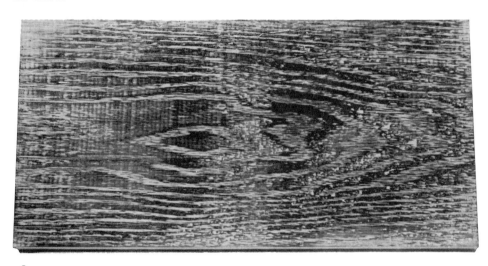

Fig. 8. Slightly scorched wood molding covered with a patina.

Fig. 9 (left). Softwood frame scribed and antiqued as described in finish No. 6.

Fig. 9A (below, left). Corner detail of the frame shown in fig. 9.

Fig. 10 (below, right). Molding scrubbed with a wire brush to remove the soft wood, and treated with a patina, as described in finish No. 7.

3

TREATMENT OF RAW-WOOD FRAMES

In this chapter we shall discuss finishes which do not hide but on the contrary utilize the texture of the wood. This type of treatment is popularly referred to as "pickling." The aim is to give the natural beauty of the grains in the wood every chance to show through the superimposed finish.

In general practice, hardwood moldings, such as a coarse-grained oak or chestnut, are best suited for these finishes. However, a softwood, such as pine or spruce, can also be used if its grain is sufficiently interesting. But a uniformly smooth, grainless wood surface should be painted with gesso (see chapter IV), as the wood itself does not possess enough character for pickling.

The coloring of the wood should be done with dry (powder) earth pigments, such as ocher, sienna, umber, ivory black, or with India ink.

As a binder for these pigments (except in the case of India ink, which does not require binding) use glue or varnish (prepared as described in chapter II). However, earth pigments may, in some instances, be mixed with water and applied. Upon drying, the color may be worked into the grain of the wood by rubbing with a piece of rag. This treatment gives a lighter color finish, but the pigment will attach itself firmly enough to the wood surface so that when a second aqueous color is required on top of the first, only very little of the original color will come off.

Dark-colored natural wood surfaces are not too attractive in themselves and are usually better finished in a light gray patina (prepared as described in chapter II).

Close-grained softwood can be colored as already described, on a smooth surface, or it can receive a different treatment. The wood can be thoroughly dampened, then rubbed strongly with a wire brush to wear the soft parts down between the grain. The resulting weatherbeaten surface is then covered with a light patina, and the protruding top grain of the wood can be tinted with umber oil color applied with a rag.

Coarse-grained hardwood can be treated by any of the preceding methods, except the last. It can also be scorched with a flame from a blowtorch, bunsen burner, or gas jet, until it attains the tone desired. Depending on the duration of the exposure to the flame, this color will range from tan to black. Patina is applied next; then, upon drying, sandpaper and steel wool should be used to remove most of the patina from the top surface, leaving it embedded in the grain of the wood. Occasionally this treatment may be given to a softwood, but it is most effective on the hard.

All surfaces treated in the manners described above should, upon drying, be rubbed with steel wool and waxed as a final finish.

A high gloss can best be produced on any gesso finish by polishing with steel wool.

Wax can also be used to obtain a higher gloss, but tests should be made on the frame in question to see whether it does not too greatly deprive the patina of its lean, matt quality. In other words, you must be careful before waxing over a patina that the wax will not either darken it too much or make it too shiny. A patina that is poor in glue content will darken under a coat of wax. The formula of one ounce of glue to one pint of water should therefore always be closely followed. When using glue of inferior quality, this proportion of glue and water will be insufficient to prevent the darkening of the gessoed surface. In such instances, increase the proportion of glue by 50 per cent or even more. (Wax will also darken a gesso poor in glue.)

*   *   *

Frame Finish No. 1

Wood: coarse-grained oak, chestnut, pine, or spruce

Materials	*Tools*
pigments: any one of the following: raw umber or burnt umber, ocher, ivory black	1 brush (2″)
	1 pan
	sandpaper (fine grade)
Copal Varnish (or casein or glue size) (see chapter II)	steel wool
wax paste (page 87)	

First step. Smooth any excessive roughness on the frame molding with sandpaper. The wood should feel quite smooth to the fingers.

Second step. Mix the pigment you have chosen (raw umber, burnt umber, ocher, or ivory black—or a mixture of more than one of these according to the shade of color desired) with Copal Varnish or glue size described under varnish color or glue color on the preceding pages. (In the case of this and all other *raw-wood moldings* excepting finish No. 3, pigment mixed with water to usual water-color consistency can be used for a lighter effect, instead of the varnish color or glue color.) Next brush the solution *thinly* onto the molding and, when it is well covered, allow to dry. Drying can be accelerated by placing in the sun or near a stove.

Third step. Sandpaper most of the color off, or, for a darker effect, allow more of the color to remain on the molding. Then polish with steel wool.

Fourth step. When thoroughly smooth, wax the frame.

Observations: This treatment wholly preserves the character and the texture of the wood, the pigment being used merely to darken the color. Should the wood already be of a rather dark color, then sandpapering and waxing alone may suffice. In general, *natural* wood of a very light color does not go well with oil paintings.

Wood should never be colored with a commercial aniline dye, for the stain will bleed through any subsequent coating and, apart from this, pigment produces a more pleasant effect than a dye.

Frame Finish No. 2 (fig. 2)

Wood: coarse-grained oak, chestnut, pine, or spruce

Materials	*Tools*
Copal Varnish (or casein or glue size) (chapter II)	2 brushes (1″ and 2″)
	2 pans
pigments: umber or ocher	sandpaper (fine grade)
gray patina (chapter II)	steel wool
wax paste (page 87)	

First and second steps. Sand and cover the molding with color as in finish No. 1 and allow to dry.

Third step. When dry, remove as much of the color as needed to bring out the texture of the wood, using sandpaper and steel wool.

Fourth step. Brush the gray patina over the entire molding. Make sure that the patina spreads down into all the crevices, corners, and carvings. While still wet, rub off most of the patina with a moist rag from the exposed profiles and ornaments, leaving the gray paint chiefly in the corners and depressions of the wood grain.

Fifth step. After the patina has dried well, sandpaper and rub the surface with steel wool to a pleasant gloss.

Observations: The color of the patina should be well considered beforehand so as to enhance the color of the wood. An identical color to the wood, for example, would be ineffective. A molding of a warm color should receive a patina of a cool tonality; a very dark wood can be treated, perhaps, with a white patina which, in fact, will be merely a *thin* white gesso. (This is described in finish No. 3.) I stated that the patina should be rubbed off while still wet. When dry, not enough of it could be easily removed by sandpapering. However, you can also wipe off a dried-in patina with a wet rag and get a good effect.

Frame Finish No. 3 (fig. 3)

Wood: coarse-grained oak

Materials	*Tools*
Copal Varnish (or casein or glue size) (chapter II)	2 brushes (1″ and 2″)
	2 pans
pigments: umber or umber and ultramarine	sandpaper (fine grade)
light gray patina (or very thin white gesso) (chapter II)	
shellac (white)	
wax paste (page 87)	

First step. Paint the molding with umber or umber and ultramarine or black glue color (or varnish color) mixed as described in chapter II. Allow to dry.

Second step. Sandpaper the molding, being careful not to take off too much color. Next, cover with shellac. Allow to dry.

Third step. Brush on a light patina (or a very thin white gesso) and rub off with a rag while still wet so that only traces of it remain in the crevices, corners, and in the grain of the wood.

Fourth step. Polish with steel wool.

Fifth step. Wax the frame.

Diagram XV.

Frame Finish No. 4 (fig. 4 and diagram XV)

Wood: wormy chestnut

Materials and tools. Use the same materials and tools as for finish No. 3.

Treat the raw wood as described in finish No. 3, from start to finish, using the umber pigment only. However, surface marked *A* in diagram XV can receive a somewhat different treatment.

Variation 1. The surface *A* can be painted in a black glue color solidly (that is, opaquely). When dry, cover with shellac. Allow the shellac to dry, then brush on the gray patina. Rub off most of the patina while it is still wet, leaving the patina in the corners and crevices of the wood surface. When dry, rub the surface with steel wool to produce a satiny gloss.

Variation 2. Instead of using the black color on surface *A*, red iron oxide glue color can be painted on opaquely. When dry, cover with shellac. Next, treat with a patina as in variation 1 and polish.

Variation 3. Gold and silver designs (on red or black grounds) such as described in chapter VII and illustrated by figs. 26–29 are especially attractive when used on such flat sections (surface *A* of a frame).

Frame Finish No. 5 (figs. 5, 6, 7, 8)

Wood: Coarse-grained oak, chestnut, pine, or spruce

Materials	*Tools*
gray patina (chapter II)	blowtorch (or bunsen burner
wax paste (page 87)	or ordinary gas range burn-
	er)
	1 brush (1″ or 2″)
	1 pan
	sandpaper (fine grade)
	steel wool

Observation: Color can be imparted to wood not only by the pigment but by the use of a flame as well. The hard woods can attain particularly glowing and deep tones from yellowish golden to deep brown and black, depending on the length of exposure to the flame. *Oak responds best* to such treatment. Wormy chestnut darkens less uniformly and softwood can easily be scorched by the hot flame. If too much black appears on the surface of any wood after it has been scorched, sandpaper will remove the excess carbon.

First step. Lean the frame against some fireproof support. A blowtorch is the best. Follow the manufacturer's directions for starting burner. Singe the molding with the flame to the desired depth of color. The scorched color effect (with the exception of black) will not always be uniform, for lighter or darker effects will be produced, depending on the length of exposure to the flame. However, the irregularity of tones contributes to the charm of the finish.

Second step. Cover the entire molding—all depressions, crevices, and corners—thoroughly with gray patina and, while still wet, rub off from the exposed profiles and ornaments. Allow to dry.

Third step. Rub with sandpaper and steel wool, then wax the frame.

Frame Finish No. 6 (fig. 9)

Wood: any kind of softwood

Materials	Tools
yellow-gray patina (chapter II)	1 brush (2″)
	1 pan
rottenstone	some pointed instrument, such
umber oil paint	as awl, nail, ice pick, file, etc.
	sandpaper

Observation: The idea of this finish is to give the frame the weathered appearance of driftwood; thus any tool capable of inflicting scars, scratching, and holes on the surface can be used. Study the illustration closely for the type of effect desired. The surface of this frame was originally smooth and unscarred. *The scratching* (or scribing, as it is professionally termed) *of the surface should run parallel to the wood grain and not across it, otherwise unpleasant effects will result. The scribing should also end at the miter—any continuation of a groove or crevice into the adjoining frame bar would ruin its appearance.* Hence, it is advisable to start the treatment from the corner toward the middle of the molding and not to work toward the corner, thus avoiding the risk of slipping into the next bar of the frame.

First step. Scribe the frame as described above with any kind of tool that will help to roughen up the molding as illustrated in fig. 9.

Second step. Cover the entire frame—all the crevices, holes, and grooves—with a patina of a warm yellowish-gray color (chapter II). Allow to dry, and sandpaper. This treatment alone, incidentally, will produce a very attractive finish and you need not go further if you don't wish to. However, the last operation (third step) is described if you are aiming at the effect illustrated in fig. 9.

Third step. Take up on a piece of rag *a little* umber oil color (taken straight out of the tube) and go lightly over the top of the wood surface. Do not force the paint into the crevices. The oil paint will then rest on the top of the ridges, which should now be dusted with rottenstone. Allow to dry, then brush off excess rottenstone.

Frame Finish No. 7 (fig. 10)

Wood: any coarse-grained wood

Materials	Tools
gray or yellowish patina	1 brush (2″)
rottenstone	1 pan
umber oil color	hard wire brush
	sandpaper

First step. The wood should be dampened for one or two hours by placing wet rags on the molding. (Wet rags are used so that you can avoid wetting the glue at the mitered corners.) Then, with a wire brush, scrub down the frame, always following the direction of the grain, until the grain protrudes sharply. The effect we are after with this finish resembles old driftwood or weathered lumber which has not been protected by paint. In stores such frames are actually called driftwood frames. A motor-driven wire brush can also be used for wearing down the soft parts of the wood, or else the wood can be sandblasted. You may be able to have this done in an automobile paint shop, where such machines are used for removing old paint.

Second step. Cover frame thoroughly with patina and let dry.

Third step. (This is optional.) Sandpaper and treat the top surface of the grain with a rag moistened with umber oil color as described in second step of finish No. 6. Apply rottenstone and, upon drying, brush off the loose powder.

GENERAL TREATMENT OF WOOD SURFACES

Although the processes hitherto described deal specifically with finishes for the picture frame, identical treatment can be accorded to a variety of objects made of wood, such as sculptures, carvings, furniture, wood paneling, etc., to produce the same graining and "antique" surface effects.

The reader may already have noticed that I have omitted any discussion of the old stand-bys in finishing wood, namely, all the oil varnishes, lacquers, and oil paint. Although these oleaginous or resinous materials can be used for some finishes, they have to be ruled out in connection with patina (or gesso) because they ruin the attractive lean appearance of the finish.

At one time frames were treated in lacquer and varnish, but this high gloss is contrary to our contemporary taste. The lean, flat character of a patina or gesso surface is its greatest charm. Hence, even wax should be used with discretion so as not to produce a fat glossy appearance. When polished with sandpaper and steel wool a patina or gesso will attain a characteristic satiny sheen which is agreeable and quite different from the gloss produced by oil varnishes or shellac.

If, however, a hardwood such as oak or chestnut, carries only traces of the patina and shows predominantly its own characteristic texture, a high gloss need not be detrimental.

I repeat that commercial aniline wood stains as sold in hardware and paint stores should not be used. Treatment with raw pigments, especially the earth colors, are preferable by far. Should any finish, whether gesso or flame treated, appear unsatisfactory, you can easily modify it. In fact one cannot "ruin" a finish, and quite often the more "messing around" that is done with the moldings, the richer or more interesting the final effect may become. Rubbing off undesirable coats of patina with a moist rag or sanding off the varnish color can lead toward producing an interesting "antique" character.

As to the finish of the sides and the back of the frame, treat these simply with varnish color or with a patina. No special effects are necessary.

4

FRAMES WITH A GESSO FINISH

The design of the molding will in large measure decide the type of finish for a frame. The diagrams and illustrations that accompany the finishes described in this chapter show suitable types of moldings for each finish.

No matter how much one particular gesso finish may differ from another, the side and back surfaces of all moldings, as mentioned before, need not be gessoed but can simply be painted with a patina of a neutral color. There is no need for any further treatment of these parts of the frame.

Gesso is a most attractive finish and is suitable, in one or another light color, for just about every painting and interior setting. Plain wood moldings and carved frames can be painted with gesso without further embellishment. Plain-surfaced frames —those without carving or too many profiles—can also be made more interesting by combing (with a common hair comb) or by adding other sculptured or textured effects as described in finishes 8 to 18 and as shown by the illustrations.*

Before we present step-by-step directions for each particular finish, here are a few general notes on the gesso treatments.

Surfaces can be gessoed, then colored with a patina. They can also be gilded as described in chapter VII.

A white gesso foundation can be *stained* with glue color or varnish color (see chapter II) or with India ink. Colors other than India ink must then be protected by a coat of shellac and the whole (upon drying) covered with patina. Sandpapering the patina-stained gesso which has been applied over the surface will bring out the underlying colors in interesting textures.

Various color effects can be produced by (*a*) glue color, varnish color, or India ink *spattered* on a gessoed surface; (*b*) glazing a white gesso foundation (which has first been made

* See information about new preparations in the Preface.

nonabsorbent by the use of shellac) with transparent gum resins, such as gamboge or dragon's blood, or else with thin glue color or varnish color mixed with burnt sienna, Prussian blue, or alizarin crimson. This will produce interesting effects. In (*a*) and (*b*) the finish *should* receive a coat of wax or, better still, resin wax (prepared from carnauba wax as described in chapter VII).

White combing or scratching on a white gesso foundation (first coat) can be colored through the application of a patina. Sandpapering will bring out the white undercolor on the raised comb marks, while steel wool will impart a sheen to the finish. In order to preserve the lean character of the finish, wax should *not* be used for polishing (unless the gesso will not be darkened by it).

Combing in gray gesso on top of a white gesso foundation (first coat) will bring out white lines in the depressions of the combing. Sandpapering or rubbing the surface with steel wool will get rid of any roughness.

Various patterns can be *impressed* on the surface of a semisoft gesso coating by brush, modeling tool, or other instrument that may be adaptable to the purpose. Or a coarse-grained piece of raw linen can be impressed upon it, then removed, leaving a weavelike texture on the gesso. Incisions on the semisoft gessoed surface made with a wooden stylus (as with the comb) will reveal the underlying color, which should contrast with the top coat. Fine scratching can also be made on a *dry* gesso surface with a sharp instrument in sgraffito technique. (See figs. 19-21 and 26.)

Although it is necessary to shellac the glue color or varnish color when superimposing a gesso or a patina, a final *gesso* finish should never be shellacked.

As to the type of wood suitable for a gesso finish, this is immaterial, for the grain will always disappear under one or more layers of gesso. Any raw-wood frame you may have or any wood molding you may buy will lend itself well to a gesso-painted finish. However, overly smooth or slick wood surfaces should be roughened with sandpaper to make the gesso adhere well.

We start with finish No. 8, a most simple and effective one. You will note that in every finish in this chapter, white gesso serves as the first coat.

Diagram XVI.

Frame Finish No. 8 (diagram XVI)

Materials	*Tools*
white gesso	2 brushes (1″ and 2″)
pigment: iron oxide red	2 pans
(powder form)	sandpaper
gray patina	steel wool
Copal Varnish or glue size	
shellac	

(Refer to chapter II for the preparation of these materials.)

First step. A layer of white gesso of a rather thick consistency should be brushed onto the molding. This means that only a little water should be added to the commercial casein paint (such as Kem-Tone, Luminall, etc., if your gesso is prepared in this way). Add just enough water so that the gesso spreads evenly over the frame without leaving heavy brush marks. This first coat when dry does not need sandpapering unless it is quite rough, in which case sand it down a little with a fine grade sandpaper. The wood surface with its color and grain pattern should disappear under this coat of gesso.

Second step. Brush red varnish color (or red glue color) on profile *X* (diagram XVI). Allow to dry, then shellac.

Third step. When the shellac is dry, brush the gray patina very thinly over the entire frame (that is, on *A, B,* and *X*). Then rub some of it off profile *X* while still wet so as to reveal the underlying red color in parts and permit the rest to dry.

Fourth step. Steel-wool profile *X* and sandpaper surfaces *A* and *B,* so that in the first instance the underlying red color and, in the second instance, the underlying white gesso reappear.

Diagram XVII.

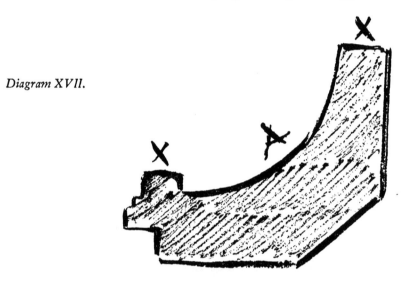

Frame Finish No. 9 (diagram XVII)

Materials	*Tools*
white gesso	2 brushes (1″ and 2″)
Copal Varnish or glue size	2 pans
pigments: umber, ultramarine,	sandpaper
iron oxide red	steel wool

(Refer to chapter II for the preparation of these materials.)

First step. Paint frame with white gesso as in finish No. 8, first step. Allow to dry. (Sandpapering optional.)

Second step. Apply red varnish color to surface *X* and umber-ultramarine varnish color (or some other neutral color combination) to surface *A.*

Third step. Upon drying, sandpaper and steel-wool the entire molding to a satiny finish.

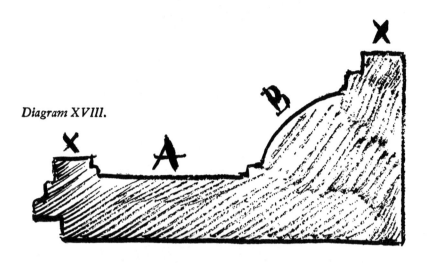

Diagram XVIII.

Frame Finish No. 10 (fig. 11, diagram XVIII)

(An identical finish can be seen in fig. 12, but the outside profile is carved and gilded.)

Materials	*Tools*
white gesso	3 brushes (two 2″, one 1″)
Copal Varnish or glue size	3 pans
pigments: umber, black and	sandpaper
iron oxide red	steel wool
gray patina	wood rasp (to notch the out-
wax paste	side and inside profiles)
shellac	

(Refer to chapter II for the preparation of these materials.)

First step. Paint the frame with white gesso as in finish No. 8, first step. Allow to dry.

Second step. Brush black glue or varnish color opaquely on surface *A*. Then paint a heavy red glue color or varnish color on profiles *X*. Allow to dry. Rub with steel wool and coat the whole frame with shellac.

Third step. Brush neutral-colored patina over the entire molding and while still wet, wipe off most of it from X and A, leaving the patina mostly in the crevices. Allow to dry.

Fourth step. Rub X and A with steel wool. Then sandpaper B so that some of the underlying color (white gesso) reappears. Wax A and X.

Observation: Instead of black, an umber or even a red color can be applied to surface A if a warmer tone is desired.

A variation of this finish can be made in the following manner: Surface X will remain as in finish No. 10 and B as in finish No. 5 for raw-wood frames. Surface X can also be treated in several different ways.

Variation 1. First step. Follow the general directions for finish No. 10, but cover surface X with black or umber varnish color or glue color.

Second step. Prepare a very light gray patina or several multicolored patina paints and spatter one or a few of these colors onto surface X. The rest of the molding should be protected from the spray. (To do this, put paper over the surfaces not to be spattered and fasten it down with cellulose tape.) The spattering is produced simply by bending back, with the finger, the bristles of a brush which has been previously dipped in the patina and aiming the spray at surface X. For such a spray the paint should be sufficiently liquid not to stick to the brush. Lastly, when dry, wax the spattered surface.

Variation 2. Surface X should be prepared to receive a gold or silver leaf as explained in chapter VII. The ground can be of iron oxide red (see "The priming of surfaces to be treated with gilt" in chapter VII) or umber. Instead of varnish, *glue (or casein) should be used as a binder for the pigment (iron oxide red or umber) because it is more suitable for the polishing which is needed in connection with gilding.* The gold can be applied in a variety of techniques and patterns.

Frame Finish No. 11 (fig. 12, diagram XVIII)

Use a frame molding of similar character to the one used in finish No. 11. But instead of black, use red color (iron oxide)

Fig. 11. Molding gessoed, then treated with glue color and patina, as described in finish No. 10.

Fig. 12. *Molding gessoed and treated with glue color. The outside profile is carved and finished in gold leaf over a red priming. A gray patina covers the whole frame.*

Opposite page:

Fig. 13 (top). *Combing wet gesso on a frame with a wide-toothed comb.*

Fig. 13A (center). *Applying color to the dried combed surface.*

Fig. 13B (bottom). *Applying a gray patina after the step shown in fig. 13A and after the color has dried.*

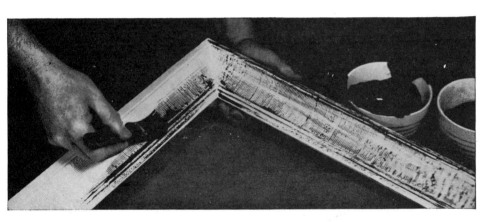

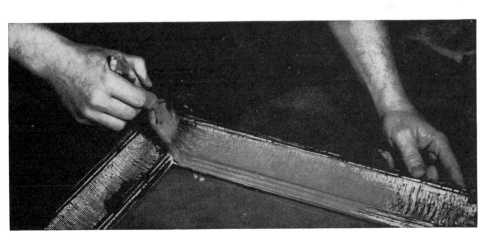

Fig. 14. Molding finished in gray gesso applied on top of white combed gesso. For method of combing see fig. 13.

Fig. 15. The flat surface of this frame shows faint comb marks. Here the first white gesso coat was covered (prior to combing) with umber and ultramarine glue color (the comb marks were scratched in on the hard surface). The outside and inside profiles were gilded with wax gilt.

Fig. 16. Molding showing very wide comb marks made in white gesso. The frame was covered with a gray patina.

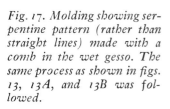

Fig. 17. Molding showing serpentine pattern (rather than straight lines) made with a comb in the wet gesso. The same process as shown in figs. 13, 13A, and 13B was followed.

Fig. 18. The pattern on this frame was produced by drawing an old razor blade, nicked in a few places, over the wet gesso. The frame was next colored and shellacked. Over this a gray patina was applied, then wiped off while still wet—leaving the patina in the crevices.

63

Fig. 19. Stippled effect made in wet gesso.

Fig. 20. Impression of raw linen applied over the wet gesso.

Fig. 21. Pattern incised with a modeling tool in stiff gesso.

to cover the flat surface of the molding (such as *A* in diagram XVIII) and the outside profile, which should be carved and gilded. This finish utilizes gold or silver leaf. The patina, as usual, is the last coat to be applied and is spread over the entire metallic surface. While still wet, the patina should be rubbed off so that only traces remain. The gold or silver will be revealed in an irregular pattern, giving the frame a sumptuous appearance.

SCULPTURED EFFECTS ON THE GESSO FINISH *

Thus far we have described a variety of finishes, most of which rely to a great extent on the effect of the wood texture. Or else we have covered the molding with a gesso or varnish color which is, as a rule, thin in character. Now we shall enliven some thick gesso finishes with sculptural effects—to which gesso lends itself particularly well. Various designs can be made in the gesso with simple instruments such as a piece of comb broken in two (separating the fine from the coarse teeth), a razor blade nicked in several places to produce irregular combing marks, a wooden stylus or a modeling tool (see fig. 1), an awl, a stiff brush (for stippling), and so on. Textured effects can also be made in the gesso by applying, then removing, a piece of extra-coarse-grained fabric, such as burlap, leaving the pattern of the material impressed on the gesso all over the frame.

Frame Finish No. 12 (figs. 14, 15)

Materials	Tools
white gesso	3 brushes (of 1″ and 2″ size)
gray gesso	3 pans
patina	combs
pigments: iron oxide red, raw	sandpaper
umber, ultramarine, ocher	steel wool
shellac	
glue size	

(Refer to chapter II for the preparation of these materials.)

First step. Paint frame with thin white gesso as in previous finishes. Allow to dry.

---

* See information about new preparations in the Preface.

Second step. Prepare a second coating of white gesso, adding raw umber or umber and ultramarine with some ocher if needed to produce an agreeable gray color, and brush generously over *one bar* (that is, one complete side) of the frame. On small frames such as 10″ x 12″, for example, all four bars can be treated simultaneously, but certainly on frames of 16″ x 20″ or larger, don't attempt to cover all the bars with gesso at once, otherwise you will find the gesso will have dried out too much on the second, third, or fourth bar by the time you are ready to perform the next operation. After a few minutes, this heavy gray gesso will start to set and acquire a thick consistency which will allow combing. The consistency should be sufficiently stiff so that the marks left by the comb will not run together; on the other hand the gesso should not be allowed to become so stiff that easy combing will be difficult. In other words, allow the gesso to dry out until it has a consistency something like butter.

Comb the gesso from the inside edge of the frame outward to achieve the effect shown in figs. 14 and 15. Next proceed to the second bar of the frame, and so on. The thicker the gesso, the deeper you can make the marks. Thin gesso will produce a faint pattern which you may prefer for some paintings (fig. 15).

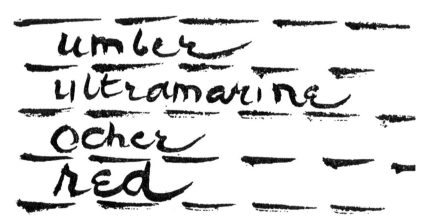

Diagram XIX. *Colors to be applied in stripes to the combed surface of molding in finish No. 13.*

When thoroughly dry, sandpaper and polish the frame with steel wool until the ridges are quite smooth. Naturally don't sandpaper so much that the combed effect is lost.

Third step. Apply red oxide priming (see chapter VII) to all the profiles that you wish to gild. When dry, sandpaper and steel-wool the surface smooth, then shellac. When the shellac dries, gild all profiles as described in chapter VII.

Fourth step. Lastly, you can color the metallic surfaces in the manner described toward the end of chapter VII, and antique the gold with a patina.

Frame Finish No. 13 (figs. 13, 13A, 13B, 16, 17 and diagram XIX)

Materials	*Tools*
white gesso	4 brushes (of 1″ and 2″ size)
gray patina	4 pans
Copal Varnish or glue size	combs (or other instruments
pigments: umber, iron oxide	described earlier in this sec-
red, ultramarine, ocher	tion)
shellac	sandpaper
(See chapter II for preparation	steel wool
of these materials.)	

First step. Apply thin white gesso to the frame (as in finish No. 12). Allow to dry.

Second step. Cover the frame bars (sides), one at a time, with the heavy second coat of white gesso and comb as described in finish No. 12. Allow to dry.

Third step. Spread the varnish colors—one at a time—in parallel rows over the combing to produce a striped effect (see diagram XIX). Allow to dry.

Fourth step. Apply red priming to the profiles which are to be gilded (see chapter VII). Sandpaper and steel-wool the surface smooth. Shellac, then gild the profiles when the shellac is dry, as described in chapter VII.

Fifth step. Spread the patina over the entire molding and, before it dries, remove much of it from the gilding.

Sixth step. Sandpaper the textured surface so as to bring out the underlying colors in spots which are more or less evenly balanced on the four bars of the frame. The surface effect of the combing will now be as seen in diagram XX and figs. 16 and 17.

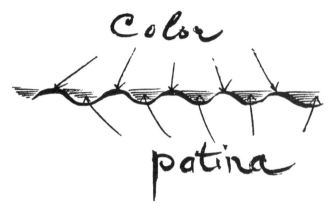

Diagram XX. Illustration showing where the colors of the molding will appear through the layer of patina.

Frame Finishes Nos. 14 and 15 (figs. 17, 18)

Materials and tools. The same will be needed as for finish No. 13.

The process for finish No. 14 is the same as illustrated by figs. 13, 13 *A*, and 13*B*. In this finish, however, the comb should be moved in a serpentine motion to produce the characteristic pattern. In finish No. 15, a nicked razor blade was used to produce the effect shown in fig. 18.

Frame Finishes Nos. 16, 17, 18 (figs. 19, 20, 21, 22)

Materials and tools. The same will be needed as for finish No. 13.

Finishes Nos. 16, 17, and 18 are all variations of the preceding technique.

Finish No. 16 (fig. 19). Instead of a comb, a brush was used to produce the stippled effect shown in the illustration. This is done in the white gesso (before it sets) by holding the brush in a vertical position and rapidly moving it up and down on the surface in a dabbing motion. The gray patina was applied on top of the dry gesso, and sandpapering of the patina (also after drying) brought out the underlying white color on the stippled ridges.

Finish No. 17 (fig. 20). Instead of using the comb or brush, this finish was produced by a piece of coarse linen pressed into the gesso before it congealed. It is more convenient to do this with a small strip of linen, pressing it onto the surface and removing it again in fairly quick motions until the whole area is thus treated.

Finish No. 18 (fig. 21). This variation shows a pattern incised or impressed upon the gesso, also before it congealed. Here a modeling tool such as shown in fig. 1 (extreme right) was used. Ornaments scratched with a sharp tool on a *well-dried* gesso are seen in figs. 26, 27, and 28.

This scratching technique is called sgraffito. The process relies on scratching the top surface of a particular color so as to allow the underlying surface, made up of a different color, to show through. For example, a design scratched into the black color will show the white of an underlying gesso. Of course, any other color combination can be used, but one should always observe the principle of scratching a thinly applied surface which rests on top of a heavier paint layer.

These are but a few suggestions of many possible sculptural treatments in gesso. After experimenting it will be up to your own inventiveness to work out other variations or new patterns using different tools such as an ornamental dye, compass (for circular designs), and so on.

GENERAL NOTES ON THE GESSO TECHNIQUE

After all the operations prior to the sandpapering have been carried out, the appearance of the finish will be far from satisfactory. But—and this seems to be the crux of the gessoing technique—sandpapering will at once unify any disjointed color effects and bring out the peculiar characteristics inherent in the gesso material. Sandpapering, in other words, gives the final touches and perfects the previous treatment.

Remember also that a matt (dull) gesso surface is always preferable to a shiny finish. A gloss on exposed surfaces such as might have been caused through frequent handling is unobjectionable but the more inaccessible parts of the molding should always remain dull.

Generally speaking, strong or dark colors should not be used for *final* effects. A light, faded appearance of the gesso is more attractive, nine times out of ten.

Mechanical perfection should not be attempted, for irregularity of the finish adds charm and interest to the surface and the effects of sandpapering enhances the texture of the whole.

Although a properly prepared gesso solution has excellent adhesive properties, when thickly applied to a nonabsorbent and overly smooth surface it may crack or pull off. Therefore, as previously stated, *a very smooth wood surface should first be roughened* with a coarse sandpaper before gessoing. Also, if two coats of gesso are applied and the undercoat has less glue than the second coat, the latter may crack.

5

THE INSERT AND ITS FINISH

Observe that in most of our frame illustrations for oil paintings, an insert has always been used. Ready-made raw-wood
frames, as a rule, do not come with inserts, but it is quite easy to
make them. The molding is simple and need not be varied. The
two designs suggested in diagram XIII will do for all types of
paintings and frames. As we established in an earlier chapter, the
insert should generally be about 1″ to 1¼″ wide, of which ¼″
remains hidden by the rabbet of the frame. On small paintings
of up to 12″ x 16″, the insert can be wider, but it should rarely
exceed 2 inches. The depth of the molding for an insert should
not exceed ½″. Where the insert meets the picture it should be
⅛″ thick.

The finish of the insert will be in gesso, or the raw-wood
molding can be covered with a raw painter's linen as seen in fig.
2 and many other illustrations in the book. How to cover the
insert with linen is described in finish No. 3 on the following
pages.

If we remember that to all intents and purposes an insert is a
frame within a frame it will be easy to see how it should be made
and placed in position. The same construction principles and
operations apply to it as to the assembling of the molding to
make the outer frame. You will find notes on mitering and joining given in chapter IX. The four strips of 1″ or 1¼″ wood
required for the insert should be mitered at each end and assembled in a square which will fit into the rabbet made for this purpose on the back of the frame proper. The insert is then nailed
in place. In measuring your frame to fit a particular canvas, be
sure to allow for the width of the rabbet in your dimensions.

Insert Finish No. 1 (fig. 14)

Materials	Tools
gesso	2 brushes (1″ and 2″)
gray patina (see chapter II)	2 pans
	sandpaper (fine grade)
	steel wool

First step. Cover the insert molding with white gesso just as you would in painting the rest of the frame. Allow to dry, then sandpaper to a smooth finish.

Second step. Brush on a patina of extra-thin consistency (or a varnish color or glue color). This should be rather lighter than the color used on the frame proper. Allow to dry and polish with steel wool. This will produce a slightly mottled appearance of the surface.

Insert Finish No. 2

Materials	Tools
gray patina (see chapter II)	1 brush (1″)
	1 pan
	sandpaper (fine grade)
	steel wool

Cover the raw-wood insert molding with a light gray patina; allow to dry, then sandpaper. The effect produced will be rather dull, which is agreeable in a narrow molding (about ½″). As a rule, I do not find this dull finish attractive on moldings of an inch or wider.

It should be noted that the color of the insert should always be lighter than the color of the frame. Sometimes an off-white or even white gessoed insert can be used.

Insert Finish No. 3 (figs. 2, 3, 8 and other illustrations showing a linen insert)

Materials	Tools
raw painter's linen	scissors
carpenter's glue	

Here we shall glue raw painter's linen to the surface of the insert. Either the linen can be glued to the four *separate* pieces of the molding from which the insert is made, or it can be glued to the insert *after* the moldings have been joined together in a square. The latter procedure is the simpler, although perhaps not quite as neat. We will describe the latter operation first:

Fixing the Linen to the Assembled Insert

First step. With a sharp pair of scissors, cut strips of linen to the length of each of the four insert molding bars (sides) after the insert has been assembled. Cut these four strips wide enough to cover not only the width of the molding, but also the entire rabbet.

Second step. Coat the walls of the entire rabbet of one bar of the insert with hot carpenter's glue (previously warmed in a double boiler or other suitable container). Press the edge of one piece of linen into the rabbet, keeping the edge of the linen even with the lower edge of the rabbet and covering the rabbet entirely. Make appropriate cuts in the linen (with scissors or razor blade) so that it will accommodate itself (diagonally) to the mitered corners of the rabbet without wrinkling. Next, apply the glue to the side and top of the insert molding, precisely from one miter to the other, and to the full width of the insert, and press the linen gently onto it. Don't extend the glue beyond the miter, also take care that the glue is not too thickly put on, otherwise it may penetrate the fabric; and stain made by the glue cannot be removed. Although such a hazard would not occur if, instead of glue, you used a library paste (such as will be recommended for making linen-covered mats), the adhesion of the material to the narrow molding of the insert will be much firmer with glue. You now have one piece of linen fastened down to one bar of the insert, including the rabbet, with loose ends of fabric only at the mitered ends of the insert.

Third step. Allow the glue to solidify, then with a razor blade and a steel rule cut the loose ends of the fabric (extending beyond the miter) precisely at and in line with the miter, that is, diagonally from the corner, at each end of the bar.

Repeat the same procedure on the adjoining bar of the insert.

Glue this side up to the miter—up to where the cloth on the first bar has been cut. Let the loose *end* of the linen of this second piece overlap the end of the first glued-on piece and, when the glue has set, cut the linen with a razor blade with the greatest possible accuracy (diagonally) exactly at the miter so it joins the first piece without any gap or overlap.

Fixing the Linen Before the Insert Is Assembled

The second, more difficult, way of attaching the fabric to the insert calls for covering each bar of the molding separately before the bars are joined together. Here four pieces of fabric are cut one inch longer than the length of each bar. The fabric is then placed over each molding, extending one-half inch beyond either end. Glue on the linen as described in the first process, and also glue the half inch of overlapping material onto the mitered sides of the molding, cutting off any surplus material. Thus, when joining the four bars of the molding to form the insert, it will be the linen-covered surfaces and not the wood which will meet at the miter. To prevent the glue from being forced out from the joints onto the linen surface when joining the moldings, apply it well below the top surface. The joining of the four pieces of molding to form the square is done with glue and with nails which should be inserted before the glue sets.

The advantage of this procedure as compared with the former is the neater appearance of the linen at the miter.

N.B. To get the linen completely flat on the inserts you can use a bone burnisher or a common kitchen spatula with dull edges. Either of these implements can be pressed over the linen to smooth out any bumps which might have appeared.

6

SUITABLE FRAMES AND MATS FOR WATER COLORS, PASTELS, DRAWINGS, PRINTS, ETC.

Frames

We have seen that for oil paintings a frame less than 2″ wide and 2″ to 3″ deep is unattractive. However, narrow and flat frames (even as narrow as 1″) can look well for water colors, drawings, etchings, prints, and other graphic work because the mat which must always be used in connection with the framing of such works counts as part of the frame.

A good average for a frame for this group of originals is between 1″ and 2½″, according to your particular taste.

The designs in diagrams III and IV indicate the general character of moldings that are suitable for framing water colors and prints. When made of a coarse-grained hardwood (oak or wormy chestnut) the moldings may be left unfinished or, if the wood appears too light, it can receive a treatment such as described in frame finish No. 2, chapter III. Raw-wood moldings, sanded and waxed, or with a slight trace of gesso, are particularly attractive for graphic work.

There is no essential difference between the gesso treatment of frames for water colors or for oil paintings. See figs. 22 and 23. In other words, the preparation of the materials for finishing raw-wood frames or gessoed frames is the same whatever the size of the molding.

Mats

Not only esthetic considerations dictate the use of a mat in framing water colors or prints, but practical thought as well, for the thickness of the mat prevents the paper surface from coming into contact with the glass. Under certain conditions enough condensed moisture may collect on the glass to spoil the picture, or at least cause the paper to wrinkle. As we know, any work executed on paper—especially in water color—will suffer when in contact with a moist surface. Paper itself can easily develop mold in the presence of prolonged high atmospheric humidity, and so does water color and pastel work.

Regardless of the size of a water color or drawing, the top and sides of the mat should never be narrower than 2½″ and the bottom 3″. But on both small and large works, the dimensions *can* be much larger if desired, according to the effect you prefer and the area on the wall you wish to cover. For proper balance, the width of the mat at the bottom should always be greater than that of the sides and the top, and in approximately the same proportions as the 2½″ x 3″ ratio given above. The reason for this is that a picture with the same area of mat at top and bottom will *appear* to have less area at the bottom. You will find the same principle demonstrated in the printed area of a double page opening in a book or a magazine, if such are well designed.

Types of Materials for Making Mats

The simplest standard mats are made from a rather thin cardboard. Thicker mats, desirable for some types of framing, can be made from fiber board which comes in ⅛″, 3/16″, and 5/16″ thicknesses. The advantage of a thick mat is that the edge surrounding the picture can be beveled and painted or finished in gold for a very fine effect. Plywood of about ½″ thickness treated with gesso can also make a very attractive matting, and so can painter's linen pasted over fiber board.

The opening of the mat (or the "window," as it is known) should always be cut on a bevel when it is ⅛″ or more in thickness. A measure of skill, or at least a very steady hand, is required for this operation, and to do it you will need a special razor-sharp knife (illustrated in fig. 1), a steel rule, and square. The cutting of mats is described in chapter VIII for those who wish to perform this operation themselves. Otherwise it can be done at your local frame or art-material shop.

The Finish of Mats

Although there is no set rule for the color of a mat in modern framing, white, ivory, light or dark gray, and black are generally the colors used for thin cardboard mats. Their surface can be smooth or pebbled. The conventional type of finish such a mat can receive is shown in fig. 24. The linear pattern is simply drawn with a pencil or a compass and India ink (of a gray-black or any desired color) and some of the areas between the lines are filled with diluted ink or a pale neutral water color. These spaces can also be gilded. The simplest way to do this is to rule up carefully and cut out strips of gilded paper to the desired width and, using library paste, stick them onto the mat. For cutting the paper, use a razor blade and a steel rule as a guide. Be sure your cutting surface is smooth and firm, such as a piece of cardboard. The ends where the strips of gilt paper meet to form the square should be cut diagonally so they fit together neatly as would the corners of a frame. Otherwise one can gild the paper (as you would gild a wood surface) with silver or gold leaf as described in the next chapter. These so-called French mats are especially suitable for graphic work done in the more conservative styles.

The material for mats sold in art-supply stores is ready for use without any additional treatment unless desired. Besides the usual plain-colored cardboard, there are also handmade papers, colored glass mats, and mirror mats and frames that you may select to give a particular print a fancy "interior decorator" type of effect. Many room settings in department stores where the pictures form part of a planned color scheme utilize such elaborate styles of framing. However, the average reader would hardly be in the position to undertake the highly skilled job of composing a mirror frame. If desired, mirror and glass mats or frames should be ordered from a frame shop, unless you can pick one up the right size at an antique dealer.

If you desire to produce special effects—in texture and color—on a mat, it is best to employ gesso on a thick fiber board. Here the bevel and the top surface should contrast in color. For example, if the top surface receives a white gesso, the bevel might be gilded. (Use the same process as when gilding a wood surface, described in the next chapter.) Or the bevel can remain with only a red priming (as used under gilt) if it suits the particular picture you are framing.

As a rule, however, the bevel should be of a lighter color than the mat. A mat painted gray might call for a white bevel, a black surface for a silver bevel, and so on, according to the colors in the picture with which it should harmonize. Here then are a few suggested finishes on thick fiber-board mats:

Finish A. A standard gesso, or patina, prepared just as you would for application on a wood surface, can be brushed smoothly on both sides of the thick fiber board. After drying, it should be sandpapered and rubbed with steel wool. A different-colored gesso or patina should then be applied to the bevel, and treated in the same manner—or the bevel can be gilded and antiqued, if you prefer, using the gilding methods described in the next chapter.

Observation: When gessoing cardboard or fiber boards, it is important to treat both sides of the board to prevent warping.

Finish B. The gessoed surface of the mat can be stippled with the end of a brush or it can show *faint* marks of the comb as described in the wood frame gesso finish No. 12. The color of the bevel should again contrast with the rest of the mat.

Finish C. The effect of this finish will rely on the superimposition of two different colors (such as gray patina on a dried white gesso or vice versa), a thin white gesso on a gray patina, or a white thin gesso on a black surface. Also varnish color or a glue color can be glazed onto the dried white gesso and, when dry, rubbed with sandpaper so as to bring out the underlying color. Such a treatment will produce effects often associated with faded, almost obliterated, ancient frescoes.

Finish D. First step. Cover the mat with a white or a yellowish gesso. Allow to dry, then sandpaper and coat with shellac. *Second step.* Select a strong color (using one or more pigments) such as burnt sienna, ultramarine, gamboge, dragon's blood (dissolved in alcohol and mixed with shellac), or any other pigment suited to the prevalent colors of the picture. Mix the color or colors either with Copal Varnish or with glue size and spread in a thin glazing fashion upon the gesso. Next, pattern the surface while still wet by dabbing with a piece of rag, a sponge, or a brush until you have an over-all textured effect. Allow to dry, then polish the mat with the carnauba resin-wax compound, the preparation of which is described early in the next chapter.

Finish E. In this finish you will have two mats, one glued on top of the other. On the first mat, made of thick fiber board, finish the bevel in gold, or in white gesso. The window of the second mat should be slightly wider so that, when glued to the first, the bevel on the first mat will show. (How to cut mats is described in chapter VIII.) Paste a raw painter's linen to the second mat (which will be much thinner than the first—approximately 3/16″ thick). For pasting the linen onto the board use white library paste. Carpenter's glue or other such liquid adhesives should not be used in this instance to avoid the danger of staining the fabric.

For pasting the linen onto the second mat (with the window already cut out) the following procedures should be observed:

Both the support and the back of the fabric should be coated with library paste, using a 2″ or 3″ brush. Don't paste over the center area of the linen (equivalent to the window in the mat) more than you can help. The fabric should then be picked up by two ends and immediately placed over the insert or mat. A rubber roller (such as is obtainable in photo stores) should next be rolled over the surfaces, working from the center toward the edges to set the linen flat. The linen covering the window of the mat is now cut out. To do this, turn the mat over and cut out the fabric in the window with a razor blade, allowing an additional inch of fabric for folding over the inside edges of the window and pasting down on the reverse side. This inch of overlap must be cut toward each corner of the window so it will fold down flat. As these ends will be hidden, it is not necessary to get an exactly even or straight cut with the blade. Brush library paste on these overlapping edges and fold them down onto the mat, using the rubber roller to get them flat.

Next, before the library paste is thoroughly dry, turn the linen-covered mat over onto its front side and glue it into position onto your first thick fiber-board mat. This time you may use a carpenter's glue. In this finish the bevel becomes separated from the linen-covered top surface, which gives the mat an especially attractive appearance as shown in figs. 22 and 23.

Frames for Etchings and Lithographs

Experience tells us that for this type of work it is best to use a raw-wood molding of oak or chestnut, as a rule not wider than 2″ and quite shallow. The molding can simply be sanded and waxed, or its color can be darkened by rubbing a dry dark pigment into its surface, this can then be covered with a light wash of patina. Any of the finishes for raw-wood moldings given in chapter III can be used for our purposes here. The mat should, as a rule, be plain and of white or ivory color, although on some occasions dark gray, or even black, mats may look well, according to your taste and also depending on where the picture is to hang and the color of the walls and the style of the room for which it is selected.

Fig. 22. A carved and combed gesso frame. The linen mat was glued onto a heavy mat with a white bevel. The wood engraving is by Dürer.

Fig. 23 (above). Another carved and combed frame in gesso finish. As in the preceding illustration, the linen mat was glued over a heavy mat with a white bevel. (Courtesy Midtown Frame Shop, New York.)

Fig. 23A (right). Detail of frame shown in fig. 23.

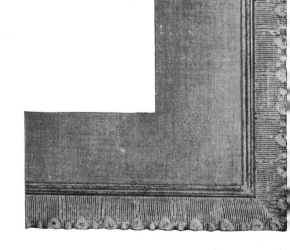

Fig. 24. French mat. The design is carried out in pencil and water color.

Fig. 25. A dark-colored gessoed mat of heavy fiber board sets off this detail from an Audubon print. The bevel is gilded and antiqued. The raw-wood frame is finished in light colors over gesso.

THE GILDING OF FRAMES

List of Materials and Tools

Here is a complete list of materials and tools needed for both procedures:

Materials for Wax-Gilt Finish

gesso (chapter II)
red priming (glue size and iron oxide)
shellac
carnauba, or resin-wax, paste (page 87)

Materials for Metal-Leaf Finish

gesso (chapter II)
red priming (glue size and iron oxide)
shellac
mordant (described next)
gold, silver, imitation gold, or aluminum leaf
patina (chapter II)

Tools

cheesecloth (for wax gilt)
brushes (1" or 2")
pans
scissors and knife (for metal-leaf finish)
gilder's tip and cushion (optional—for gold leaf)
sandpaper (fine grade)
burnisher (optional—for gold and silver leaf)
steel wool

There are two methods of gilding which concern us—*wax gilt* and *metal leaf*. Wax gilt is the simplest method and is satisfactory for most purposes. However, it is not as versatile as the traditional metal-leaf applications which can be patterned and colored with gamboge and dragon's blood. The latter are dry powders soluble in alcohol and shellac and they are obtainable from the sources described at the end of the book, if your local art-supply store does not stock them. Metal leaf can also be antiqued with a patina, whereas wax gilt cannot. But, unless you plan to further embellish the gold frame as just described, I certainly recommend that you use the wax-gilt finish.

PROFILES TO BE GILDED

Before describing in detail the techniques of gilding, we must remember which parts of the molding are the ones best suited for this treatment. This question was discussed in chapter I and various examples can be seen in the illustrations of gilded frames, such as in figs. 12, 26, 27, 28, 29, 30, 31. We must also consider the preparation of the surface to receive the gilding.

THE PRIMING OF SURFACES TO BE TREATED WITH WAX GILT OR METAL LEAF

Flat or rounded surfaces to be primed for a wax gilt or a metal-leaf gilt should be perfectly smooth. Except in the rarest instances, metal effects do not look well on rough surfaces. So the first step is to sandpaper and rub the molding with steel wool. Next, the surface must be primed to take the gold.

Although one frequently finds on some antique or commercial frames a yellow ocher and also sometimes a white ground under the gold applications, red color (iron oxide red) is, in my opinion, the most suitable for our purposes. And for silver leaf, umber or black is quite an effective priming. *In either instance the pigments should be bound by glue and not varnish because the latter does not lend itself well to polishing.* For preparing this glue-size binder, use the standard formula of glue: 1 ounce of glue to 1 pint of water. Add enough pigment to produce a rather heavy paste. The priming should be sufficiently heavy to permit thorough sandpapering and smoothing. After the priming is dry and has been well polished, give it a coat of shellac. After the shellac dries, apply the wax gilt as described earlier in this chapter. Or, if metal leaf is to be used, after shellacking it is necessary to cover it with a mordant to hold the metal leaf as described in the following pages.

THE WAX-GILT METHOD

This very satisfactory method of gilding employs carnauba

wax as a binder for bronze (gold) powder. The powder should, incidentally, be of the lightest color obtainable. (It comes in small bottles or jars.) The wax is taken up on a piece of cheesecloth, dipped in the gilt, and applied over the priming. The details of applying wax gilt follow the next few paragraphs on the preparation of carnauba wax.

Preparation of Carnauba Resin-Wax Paste for Wax Gilding

Carnauba wax is available by the pound in chunks (see sources of supply at end of book if your local art-supply store does not stock it). The preparation of the wax paste either as a binder for the bronze powder or for use in general waxing of frames is as follows:

Chip off some of the wax into small particles by means of a knife. Because carnauba wax is a hard and brittle substance quite unlike beeswax, and its melting point is much higher, it will not, like the former, dissolve in a solvent (turpentine or mineral spirits) when cold. Therefore, the material, reduced to small particles as described above, should be placed in a small tin container and heated on a hot plate until it liquefies. To avoid combustion, it is best not to work over an open flame.

The formula for this resin wax is in the proportion of 1 ounce of wax to 3 ounces of turpentine and 3 ounces of Copal Varnish. Place 1 ounce of wax in the container and warm over a hot plate. As soon as the wax has melted, add 2 or 3 teaspoonfuls of turpentine and stir well (a larger quantity of the cold solvent would make the melted wax congeal quickly). Now the compound can be taken off the electric heater and a little more turpentine added gradually; then the rest of the 3 ounces of turpentine should be poured in. After stirring, add 3 ounces of Copal Varnish. (See list of materials, page 24.) The compound will now solidify quickly.

Besides being used for gilding, the paste, as mentioned before, is of great value for *all waxing purposes,* and can be used to advantage instead of the conventional beeswax.

How to Apply Wax Gilt

The process of gilding is most simple. A little of the carnauba wax prepared as described in the preceding paragraphs should be taken up on a cloth (cheesecloth is best), dipped into a small heap of bronze powder poured out of its container into a plate or other flat-surfaced receptacle set aside for the operation, and rubbed onto the shellacked, red-primed surface of the wood. Use sufficient bronze to produce the desired sheen (more or less according to your taste). When the wax has been applied to the frame, immediately polish with a clean cloth to a high gloss until no trace of the bronze comes off. Once the varnish wax paste dries, it cannot be polished. Should this happen, you will find that turpentine will clean it off down to the priming, ready for a new start. Not only is the wax-gilt finish most effective but it is also extremely durable. Protected by the resin wax which envelopes the particles of the metal, the bronze will not tarnish or come off.

There is no adequate substitute for carnauba wax. But in an emergency one can use ordinary automobile Simonizing wax thinned a little with Copal Varnish. Such a compound, with the gold-bronze powder mixed in with it, should be left on the molding for at least 15 minutes before polishing.

The resin-wax paste should be kept in a well-closed jar where it will remain in good condition for years. The carnauba wax preparation not only is superior to any other compound employing bronze powder, but it is also extremely economical to use; one ounce of the wax will provide enough paste for literally dozens of frames.

To avoid possible confusion when reading the ensuing notes on finishing with metal leaf, it should be stated clearly that *no mordant* is used on frames that are to be wax gilded. Otherwise the preparation of the surface of the frames is the same. Step-by-step procedure for the wax gilt, then would be as follows: (1) Apply white gesso (if raw-wood molding is being used). Upon drying, polish with sandpaper. (2) Prime the surface with red iron oxide glue priming. Allow to dry. (3) Sandpaper and polish with steel wool. (4) Shellac and allow to dry. (5) Apply the wax gilt as described above. *Do not* try to tint or cover the wax gilt with a patina.

MORDANT (for metal-leaf finishes)

This is the term for the adhesive that *attaches the metal leaf* to the shellacked priming. As stated, it is used only for the metal leaf and not in connection with the wax gilt previously described. It is best to use an oil mordant such as a synthetic gold size or japan size, both of which are sold ready for use in hardware or paint stores. Even a common floor varnish with a drier (such as japan drier) can serve for this purpose quite well.

The mordant should be applied thinly on the dry shellacked surface and the gold metal placed over it when it is almost dry and merely retains a slight tack. Some of the mordants, such as the synthetic size, dry rapidly, so that in a few minutes one can commence to gild the frame.

The mordant must dry well to the touch before any manipulations, such as polish with steel wool or treating with the gum resins or patina, are carried out on top of the gilding.

SOLID-GOLD FINISH WITH METAL LEAVES

It is not our aim to produce an even, perfectly coherent gilded surface for the finishes featured in this book. However, sometimes a solid mechanically perfect gold surface is desired, and this should be done with metal leaf. Handling of gold leaf, even by the inexperienced, *can* be relatively simple, for it is perfectly in order to place even small bits of crumpled pieces of metal leaf on the profiles or the ornaments of the molding. When pieced together to cover the frame and when pressed down, they will form a solid surface, and no subsequent operations, such as are later described to obtain an "antique" effect, need be applied, although the frame will need burnishing or either shellacking or waxing according to which type of leaf is used.

To produce such a solid and even gilt surface by means of complete leaves (as they come off the book) you will find takes considerable skill. The amateur gilder will, therefore, more likely than not, "mess up" the large leaves before he succeeds in placing them on the molding, and he will resort to piecing them together on the frame as described above. However, here as in all other manual operations, skill comes with practice. The actual handling of gold leaf will be described in the following pages.

Imitation gold leaves can also be used for flat solid finishes and, like genuine gold leaf, when pressed gently onto the mordant-treated surface of the frame with the fingers, will merge so as to form a coherent surface. *Genuine gold leaf* can be burnished to a high gloss by means of a burnisher which is generally made of agate or an animal tooth and is available in better artist material stores. A high luster on an *imitation gold leaf* can, however, be achieved only by the use of shellac, wax, or still better, a resin-wax (carnauba wax) paste.

For the solid effect described above, then, follow the step-by-step instructions for applying metal leaf which are given shortly, but instead of antiquing with a patina, simply burnish the gold surface, if genuine gold leaf has been used, or shellac or wax it as described for the imitation leaf.

COMPARISON OF THE DIFFERENT METAL LEAVES AVAILABLE

Imitation gold leaf is more economical to use than *genuine gold leaf* and, since it is much heavier in weight than the latter, you will find it far easier to handle. In fact it can even be picked up with the fingers, placed directly on the primed surface of the frame and smoothed down with the fingers or a cotton tampon. *Silver leaf* is more delicate than imitation gold but sturdier than genuine. It can be cut with scissors and it can be handled with the fingers. Since its color can also be modified with gamboge, dragon's blood, or orange shellac, it is very versatile. It will tarnish unless protected with shellac. However, when tarnished with sulphur and colored with gum resins, it takes on somewhat the appearance of antique gold. *Aluminum leaf* is just as heavy as the imitation gold material (that is, heavier than silver leaf) and can be applied to the frame in the same way. It cannot be burnished like gold and silver leaf but it can be made to appear like the latter when etched with sulphur and colored with gamboge, dragon's blood, or orange shellac. Aluminum leaf lends itself well to antiquing. There is not much advantage in using aluminum leaf instead of silver except that it is a little cheaper and, with its greater thickness, easier to handle.

For most gold finishes, the amateur frame-maker who shuns any extra effort can very well limit himself to the use of *wax-gilt* alone. At any rate, there is no compelling reason for using true gold leaf if the final finishes recommended in variations *A* and *B* (shortly given) are followed. The patina and glazes which look so well when applied over metal leaf, giving it an antique appearance, will make the imitation gold leaf, for all practical purposes, indistinguishable from the genuine article.

STEP-BY-STEP PROCEDURE IN APPLYING METAL LEAF ON THE PRIMED SURFACE OF A FRAME

The metal leaves are sold in book form (about 5" square) placed loose between sheets of thin paper bound in a book. With the exception of genuine gold leaf, *they should be cut with the paper* to the desired shape (for instance, to the width of the molding or profile to be gilded) *with scissors.*

Genuine gold leaf, however, must be cut *with a knife.* To be done properly, gold leaf should be picked up from between the papers with a knife (any ordinary, not-too-sharp kitchen knife with a straight blade can be used) and placed on a so-called gilder's cushion (diagram XXI). The cushion is made of a wood panel, about 6" x 10", covered with chamois leather and stuffed with layers of cotton.

Small pieces of gold leaf can be picked up with a large, flat sable brush or a gilder's tip (diagram XXI) and then placed on the molding which has been treated with the mordant. The gold should be pressed in place with a cotton tampon. When a solid gold surface is required, each piece applied should overlap the last piece so that no joints are visible. The extra thickness thus caused is infinitesimal and it will disappear when the finish is

Diagram XXI. Gilder's cushion and tip. (N.B. The handle of the tip is usually made of cardboard and the hair of a soft variety. The gilder's cushion is homemade, as described in the text—the tip is available at art supply stores.)

burnished or when you rub over the finish with your finger.

For gilding larger surfaces, gold leaf is best used as follows: Pick up the book containing the leaves—with the thumb on top and the index finger underneath it. Beginning at the outside edge of the mordant-treated frame, apply the leaf by bending the book slowly forward, until the leaf covers the profile. Now, with a soft cotton tampon in the other hand, press the leaf down. Let the next leaf overlap the first by about ¼" and proceed thus until the entire frame is covered. The overlapping material (also that at the corners of the frame and over the edges) can be carefully wiped off and saved for future use.

The gold leaf can be polished to a high luster with a burnisher. However, when we leave it unburnished, it can be tinted with dragon's blood, whereby it attains a very beautiful deep red color. In either case a patina or glaze, or both, can be added for an antique effect.

When using imitation gold leaf, silver leaf, or aluminum leaf (which is to silver what imitation gold is to genuine gold leaf) you would proceed as follows: Cut it with the interleaving paper to the desired shape and flip it off the bottom paper onto the frame, treated with mordant. Considerable practice is required to perform this operation skillfully. The amateur gilder might just as well use his fingers.

Variation A for Metal Leaf with Antique Effect

For either gold or silver leaf,* the preparation of the frame is

_____
* Imitation gold leaf or aluminum leaf can also be used.

92

Fig. 26. *The gilded and antiqued profiles and ornaments on this frame are accented with sgraffito lines in a simple but effective pattern of squares and diamonds scratched into the flat center panel.*

93

Fig. 27A. Detail of frame shown in fig. 27.

Fig. 28. The profiles of this frame are in combed gesso. The central design is in antiqued gold accentuated with sgraffito lines. (Painting and frame by Donald Pierce.)

Fig. 27 (opposite page). Gilded and antiqued profiles with a central gilt contour design accented by sgraffito.

95

Fig. 29. Frame in raw-wood (wormy chestnut) finished in a light gray patina. The central zig-zag design is in silver leaf antiqued with sulphur.

the same, except for the color of the priming which was explained earlier in this chapter.

First step. Apply white gesso to the raw-wood molding (as in earlier finishes). Allow the gesso to dry. Polish well with sandpaper.

Second step. Apply the red iron oxide priming described earlier in this chapter. (If silver leaf is used, apply umber or black priming.) Allow to dry. Next, sand and polish with steel wool, then cover with shellac. Allow to dry.

Third step. Brush a mordant over the dry shellac, then place on it gold or silver leaf as described in the preceding pages. Allow to dry.

Fourth step. Polish the gilt carefully with steel wool and tint with one of the gum resins if desired.

Fifth step. Cover the metal leaf with a gray patina while still wet, and, wipe it off the top surface of the profiles with a moist rag. On a silver leaf, a light-colored patina, as a rule, is ineffective. Here it is best to allow the dark (black or umber) underlying surface to show through in spots after rubbing the silver leaf with steel wool. Use a patina which contrasts with the silver colors, such as white mixed with ivory, black, or ocher; or a darker shade of umber mixed with white can provide such contrasting colors. Wipe off the patina while still wet as described above.

Variation B for Gold with Antique Effect

First step. Apply white gesso on the frame as in variation *A*. Sandpaper when dry, then shellac.

Second step. Paint on a coat of black glue color. Allow to dry, then sandpaper, to bring up traces of the white gesso ground under the black.

Third step. Shellac the frame and allow to dry.

Fourth step. Apply a thin coat of red paint. Allow to dry, then steel-wool to reveal shades of the underlying colors (white and black) in parts.

Fifth step. Gild the surface (with gold leaf, imitation gold, or wax gilt), and allow to dry. *N.B.:* For gold leaf or imitation gold leaf don't forget first to apply the mordant. Next steel-wool the surface again to bring out in varying degrees all the underlying coats (white, black, red), leaving the gold in traces all over the frame. This produces an extraordinarily rich effect.

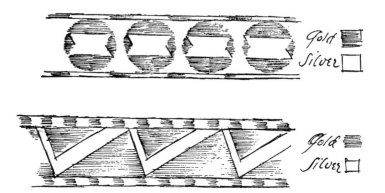

Diagram XXII. Suggested design patterns in gold and silver leaf.

Ornaments in Gold and Silver Leaf (figs. 26, 27, 28, 29, diagram XXII)

Simple as well as intricate designs in gold and silver leaf (as illustrated in figs. 26 to 29) can be produced even by the inexperienced amateur gilder. The following is the step-by-step procedure:

First step. Cut a piece of thin semitransparent paper (so-called detail paper) to the width (but not necessarily the length) of the surface to be gilded. Draw on the paper the pattern you wish to transfer to the frame. It can be a very simple pattern such as a leaf or geometric ornament shown in diagram XXII or in figs. 26, 27, 28, 29, or some good traditional design.

Second step. Rub onto the reverse side of the paper some zinc white or titanium white pigment (usually sold in artist supply stores) and place the paper on the red-primed surface of the frame. Next, trace over the design with a pencil. This will impress the white marks onto the red priming beneath. The transfer can also be made with black carbon paper. If you are using a design that repeats itself and have drawn this but once on a small piece of semitransparent paper, repeat the tracing process until the design is marked over the entire frame.

Third step. Use a mordant of a consistency that will permit easy application with a sable brush and paint the inside area of your ornaments on the frame.

Fourth step. Cover the entire molding, piece by piece, with the metal leaf and press it into place with a tampon of cotton or your finger. Allow the mordant to dry, then wipe off the loose leaf with a piece of cotton. The metal will adhere only to the surface which has been painted with the mordant.

Glazing and Tarnishing Metal-Leaf Surfaces

Whereas wax gilt cannot be treated in any fashion once it is applied, except for a polish with steel wool, metal leaf can, as I have mentioned, receive a patina to give it an antique look (see variation *A* on page 92). Before applying the patina (prepared in the same way as for all the previous frame finishes), the appearance of the gold leaf can be changed and enhanced by various manipulations. For example: To deepen the color of gold, glaze it with orange shellac, gamboge, or dragon's blood (see next paragraph), or a mixture of all three. Glazing here simply means painting the frame thinly with this material, which will allow the gold to show through. Silver leaf can be made to look like a bright gold when glazed with a mixture of orange shellac and gamboge.

These ingredients—gamboge or dragon's blood (the first yellowish, the second reddish in color)—come in powder form and should be first dissolved in alcohol to a thick pastelike consistency. Then either one or a combination of both should be mixed with white or orange shellac to a thin consistency and applied to the gold or silver or aluminum leaf with a sable brush.

Since silver and especially aluminum metal do not look well in a new condition, it is advisable to tarnish them before glazing. This is best done with sulphur powder mixed with water and applied to the metal leaf on the frame. Depending on the degree of the tarnished effect desired and the atmospheric temperature, this etching can take up to several hours. An average time would be about two hours, whereupon the sulphur should be carefully removed with a soft rag and its further action immediately stopped by coating the surfaces with shellac. Very beautiful mottled silver and aluminum effects can be produced in this manner. A surface protection of the metals (we do not speak of gold, of course) with shellac *is essential* to inhibit further tarnishing.

GENERAL NOTES ON GILDING

For best effects, the priming for any of the above metal leaves should be red, brown, or black (using the last two colors for silver- or aluminum-leaf finish). The priming should always be smoothed with steel wool and then isolated by a coat of shellac, otherwise it will absorb the mordant which is next applied to hold the leaf.

The mordant must be permitted to dry partially so as to leave only a slight tack, which is sufficient to hold the leaf in place. It is not feasible to place the leaf on a wet or even a semiwet surface.

Before any manipulations, such as burnishing, etching with sulphur, treating with steel wool, tinting, or covering with patina, are carried out, the leaf covered mordant should be permitted to dry overnight.

The sequence of operations after gilding *with metal leaf* and the drying out of the mordant is as follows:

1. Gentle rubbing with steel wool.

2. Tinting with gamboge, dragon's blood, orange shellac, or a combination of any of these ingredients, if a mottled color effect over the shiny metal is desired, as described on page 99. This and the next step are optional.

3. Covering with patina and wiping off the patina so that it stays only in the depressions of the surface to give an antique effect.

4. Waxing (either with standard commercial wax or, still better, with the carnauba resin-wax paste described early in this chapter.)

N.B.: The finest grade of *steel wool* should be used and rubbed in parallel strokes, not in circular motion; *always* polish with the grain and not against it, and do it as gently as possible.

The *shellac* when used as the binder for the coloring matter (gamboge, dragon's blood) should be of standard solution (out of a can) reduced by half with alcohol. This concentration is sufficient to bind the gum resins.

All metal leaves, with the exception of true gold leaf and aluminum leaf *must be protected by a final coat of shellac* (with or without coloring matter). Genuine gold can also be shellacked but this is not necessary as it will not tarnish like the other metal leaves.

Patina should be applied only to dry surfaces and wiped off from the gilding *thoroughly* or else the finish will appear too dull.

When the genuine gold leaf is used, traditional gesso should be prepared from white gilder's clay or the red or yellow clay pastes ground in water; these are sold under the trade name *Heins*. The pastes must be well mixed with size (glue 1 oz., water 1 pt.) to a brushable consistency before they are used.

Tissue-backed Gold Leaf

Every amateur finds the experience of handling gold leaf quite difficult. However, it is now possible to get gold leaf that is attached to tissue paper and can be easily cut with scissors and applied to the frame. This is known as *Swift Patent Gold.* As a mordant for this leaf, gellified size should be rubbed thinly onto the frame with the fingers. Next, the tissue-backed gold leaf should be pressed face down on the assigned place and the tissue paper then pulled off the surface. A satisfactory gold finish can thus be more easily obtained.

8

CARVING OF ORNAMENTS ON A FRAME MOLDING (figs. 30, 31, 32)

Since this book is primarily designed for the lay frame maker and not for a skilled craftsman, only the simplest carving operations on plain-surface moldings will be described in this chapter.

Instruments needed for carving are shown in fig. 1. Your requirements will be one flat and two or three round rasps, two or three gouges up to ½″ in width, and some sandpaper.

The use of the tools is as follows: The flat rasp will serve to round off corners and smooth the outside edges of the molding whenever this is desired. The round rasps can be used for carving with very little effort, but only on the outside profile (the one farthest from the picture). On inside profiles or on planes between profiles, only the gouge can be used. The simplest type of carving, or notching, with these instruments is shown on the frame in fig. 11.

Mastering the use of a gouge for carving simple ornaments is not very difficult. Some preliminary practice, however, on scrap pieces of moldings is advisable, as so much is dependent on getting the "feel" of the tool.

For better control and cleaner cuts, the gouge should be struck with a mallet rather than pushed with the palm of the hand. The cutting edge of the gouge must always be razorlike in sharpness, otherwise you will never get good results.

Suggestions for Carving (see diagram XXIII)

1. Mark off 1″ intervals on the profile of the molding. With the gouge held at a 60° angle to the flat surface, notch each one of the markings all around the frame with one tap of the mallet —halfway through the inner side of the profile, to achieve the semicircular depressions shown in the diagram. Sandpaper smooth.

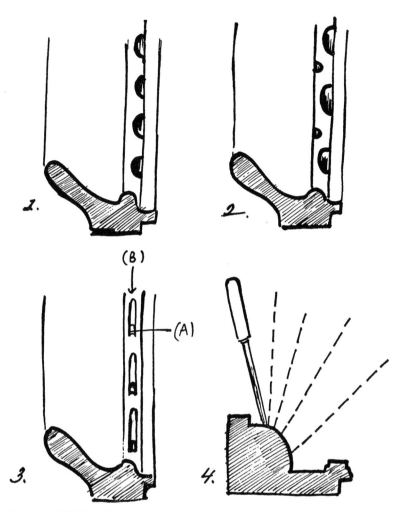

Diagram XXIII. Illustration showing the use of a gouge on moldings, and the finished result.

2. Mark off 1″ intervals on the profile and notch as in example 1, halfway through the inner side with a larger gouge. Then notch halfway through on the other side of the same profile with a smaller gouge, at even spaces between the first row of depressions. See diagram XXIII. The size of the gouges used will depend on the size of the molding, but the carving should be in about the same proportion as shown in diagram XXIII. Sandpaper the rough edges.

3. After marking off 2″ intervals all around the center of the inner profile, cut the marks (*A* in the diagram) with the gouge held vertically and with one tap of the mallet. Then complete the motif with cut *B*, holding the gouge at about a 60° angle to the flat surface, and using perhaps two or three taps of the mallet to carve out the cartridgelike shape illustrated. Sandpaper any rough edges.

4. Gouge a groove into any carved surface of a molding, bend the wrist to allow the instrument to maintain a constant degree of angle to the carved surface as represented by the position of the gouge in the diagram.

Undoubtedly after some experimentation you will work out other variations of this simple method of carving. It is very easy to do and adds much to the total effect of the frame. Slight variances in shape or size of the carvings will not matter as they will add to the handmade appearance, and they can be minimized under a gesso finish.

Machine-Made Ornaments (fig. 32)

Machine-made ornaments, such as fancy beadings of various sizes and shapes (used on period reproduction furniture), can be quite useful in making up an interesting frame. I refer to the kind obtainable at some of the better carpenter's or cabinetmaker's supply stores. One or more long strips can be cut into shorter lengths to fit the design of your frame, mitered at the corners for a neat joint, and glued onto the four sides of the molding. They usually look better if, after being attached to the frame, they are worn down a little along the beading with a rasp or coarse sandpaper to deprive them of that uniform, machine-made look. They can then be gessoed, gilded, and covered with a patina in the usual fashion. The frame illustrated in fig. 32 has such a beading. After being glued to the frame, the beading was thoroughly sandpapered and covered with patina so as to look as if it were part of the original molding.

REFINISHING OLD FRAMES

Several of the pictures you own may be suffering from old

Fig. 30. Frame finished in combed gesso. The inside profile is carved and gilded.

Fig. 31. Frame finished in combed gesso. The outside profile is carved and gilded. (The picture used for demonstration purposes is a reproduction from a Dürer water color.)

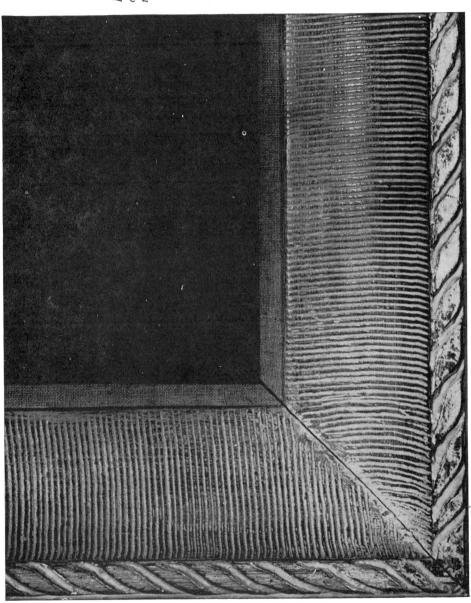

Fig. 32. The commercial bead ornament shown toward the center of
this frame was glued to the molding and treated with a gouge to make
it less mechanically even. The whole frame was covered with a patina
and sanded. Linen was glued over the insert before joining.

Fig. 33. An oil painting attached to the rabbet of the frame by means of metal strips. A corrugated board screwed onto the stretcher protects the canvas. The hole in the center of the board permits free circulation of air.

Fig. 34. Two typical examples of Barbizon frames employing traditional patterns. The making of such frames cannot be attempted by the amateur. (Courtesy Leo Robinson, New York.)

Fig. 35. Frames made of papier mâché with Baroque patterns. (Courtesy Leo Robinson, New York.)

Fig. 36. An old oval frame mounted within a square black frame with decorations painted over the gesso background makes a striking trompe-l'oeil *by Eugene Berman.*

frames that are in need of refinishing to show their contents up to the best advantage, or you may recently have bought a collection of frames at an auction sale with the object of using them for framing paintings or prints that have long been stored away.

It is quite an easy matter to refinish old frames. If any of them has an undesirable gesso finish, this can be removed with water or, if obstinate, with sandpaper. Varnished surfaces will yield to turpentine or benzine. Cracked or worn gilding can be sanded off. Oil or varnish paint can be removed from a frame with paint remover, and wood darkened by stains or age can be bleached with a commercial wood bleach or a Clorox solution. Imperfect carving or chipped-off pieces can be reconstructed with thick gesso or filled in with plastic wood.

As a matter of fact, one can endlessly experiment with new effects on old moldings while in the process of rubbing or sanding them down. More often than not, the accidental effects which result from the refinishing can make a frame appear richer and more "antique." Many an old frame, while being sanded for a refinish job, has disclosed an interesting color texture which, with the addition of a few dabs of varnish color, gesso, or a patina, has resulted in an interesting frame.

Antique frames such as may be found in secondhand shops can be made useful through refinishing, provided that the style (ornamentation) is acceptable for your purposes. If the old frame is finished in lacquer, varnish, or metal leaf, it must be well cleaned and sanded before applying gesso or any other finish. This is to make the gesso, varnish color, or glue color adhere, which it will only do on a rough or slightly absorbent surface. Painting done straight on the slick surface of an old frame will usually chip off or be otherwise marred.

A satisfactory finish in gold leaf (in other words, a gold frame in good condition) can often be made more acceptable to contemporary taste simply by rubbing it down with steel wool and then applying a gray patina in the manner described in earlier chapters.

If you have one or two old frames or broken pieces of molding, try out some of the finishes described in this book and keep experimenting. You will be surprised at what effects you can get and how you can completely transform the appearance of a picture simply by giving it a new and contemporary-looking frame finish.

AFFIXING PAINTINGS TO FRAMES OR MATS

Oil Paintings

The common practice of hammering a nail through the picture stretcher and into the back of the frame, or driving a nail into the frame and then bending it to hold the stretcher, is improper, to say the least. The best way is to attach a short copper or steel strip (the first can be bent with the fingers, the second with pliers whenever the stretcher and frame are not exactly flush with one another) by means of screws, one end of the strip being fastened to the frame and the other to the stretcher (see fig. 33). These metal strips are sold in foot lengths. They have screw holes ½″ apart and are generally available in hardware stores. They can be cut to shorter lengths with tin snips or electrician's pliers. Use a gimlet to make the holes in the stretcher and the frame before inserting the screws.

The back of the canvas of an oil painting should always be protected with a cardboard as seen in fig. 33. Use small screws and washers to affix the board to the stretchers, and make one or several openings in the board to permit free air circulation.

Water Colors, Drawings, etc.

All works done on paper, such as drawings, water colors, and prints, should be placed on a firm piece of white cardboard and attached *at the top corners only* with Scotch tape. This tape will serve as a sort of hinge, leaving the other edges free. This is necessary because paper, being hygroscopic, will react to moist and dry atmosphere, and a certain amount of shrinkage and expansion, no matter how slight, must be allowed for. If attached at all four corners, the paper, unless it is of a very heavy quality, may easily wrinkle. Over the mounted drawing or print will next go the mat, which will have an opening cut to the size of the illustration or that part of it which is to show in the framed picture. This in turn will be assembled with the glass into the frame.

SOLID MOUNTING OF WATER COLORS, PHOTOGRAPHS, COLOR REPRODUCTIONS, ETC.

All original works are normally affixed with the tape hinge just described so they can easily be removed, restored, or remounted. However, certain occasions demand that the picture be mounted solidly on a rigid support. For instance, a drawing or print may be slightly creased or torn, in which case the loose mounting previously described will not be practical. Also when framing color reproductions which are not to go behind glass, or photographs, the print should be firmly pasted down to a stiff board or other type of backing, as it is usually too hard to handle any other way. This solid mounting can be done with several adhesives, such as library paste, rubber cement, or by dry mounting.

1. *Library paste.* For general purposes of mounting paper to a firm support, library paste is the most practical medium. This excellent adhesive is also preferable for attaching linen, muslin, velvet, or other fabrics to wood or cardboard inserts or mats as in finish *E,* chapter VI. The dense paste should be placed in a small dish and reduced to a creamy consistency with a little water. It is important that all lumps be dissolved as these would otherwise show on the finished surface.

Both the paper to be mounted and the support should be coated thinly with the paste, using a stiff brush of appropriate size. It is important that the paste be spread evenly, and no excess of it should be left on either of the surfaces. To press the paper onto the support while still moist, it is best to use a rubber roller (such as is obtainable in photo stores). The roller should be rolled over the surface, working from the center toward the edges. Immediately wipe off any excess paste that may ooze out. To flatten out badly creased areas, a laundry iron can be used. A bookbinder's bone is useful to press down the paper.

2. *Rubber cement.* This adhesive should be used for temporary mounting only (it may last for a few years), as its binding properties are not permanent. It is particularly suitable for photographs and is a quick and easy way of mounting them temporarily. Both the photo and the mounting board are given a thin even coat of the cement. After a few seconds both will be dry. The photo is then picked up and one edge is carefully attached in exact position, then it is rolled back and smoothed down, first with the hands, then with a rubber roller (available at photo supply stores) to make it entirely smooth and firm. It is a good idea to have the mounting board larger than the photograph so that it may be cut square to the photo after it has been mounted. The dry, excess rubber cement can be removed from around the edges by rubbing briskly with the finger, rubber eraser, or a piece of cloth.

3. *Dry mounting.* This process involves the use of dry mounting tissue (obtainable in photo supply stores) and pressing with a warm iron. Except for small papers this method is impractical without a special, large, electric hot press. For small work, of up to 10″ x 12″, however, it produces excellent results. The dry mounting tissue is placed, single thickness, over the entire area between the backing (support or mount) and the work to be mounted. The paper to be mounted is then carefully placed in position and several sheets of ordinary paper (newspaper, writing paper, or any other soft paper) are placed on it to form a cushion. The whole is then gone over with a hot iron, working from the center out to the edges. The iron should be medium hot—not merely warm, nor so hot that it scorches the cushion of paper. This process will produce an attachment which is both smooth and permanent.

After mounting paper (or cloth on mats), it is necessary to place the work under a press of some sort for a few hours. With the work lying on a flat surface, and with a piece of protective paper covering it, place a large drawing board (or any smooth-surface board) over it and weigh it down with a heavy object —a pile of books, etc. This will provide sufficient pressure.

CUTTING MATS

The amateur mat cutter must not expect to produce a professional job the first time he tries. It takes skill and practice to cut a beveled edge in a cardboard with exact precision. My advice is to practice cutting several odd pieces of board first until you get the hang of it.

In cutting cardboard, a suitable knife is of first importance; it must have a thin, pointed edge, of razorlike sharpness. Because frequent sharpening of the blade will be essential (as explained later), it is best to work with an instrument equipped with an adjustable blade, such as is seen in fig. 1. You can also use the type of knife that is sold with a stiff razor blade affixed, though the knife mentioned above is firmer and does a better job, in my opinion. Besides the knife, a good, heavy metal ruler with beveled edge and a pencil compass are all the tools needed.

These are the salient points of procedure:

(1) Measure the area of the picture which is to show through the window of the mat, then establish exactly the width of the mat on all sides. The sides and top will be equal and the bottom will be wider (see chapter VI). Next draw the outline of the window on the mat board. This is best done by scribing. Be sure that the mat is square. Hold the pointed prong of the compass at the outer edge of the board and allow the leg with the pencil to mark the window. Keeping the pointed prong pressed against the outer edge of the mat, slide it along the edge, simultaneously letting the leg with the pencil mark a line on the mat. Mark the top and the sides to the same measure. Then increase the reach of the compass by at least half an inch (or considerably more, depending on the over-all size of the mat), and mark the bottom side in the same manner. Thus a correct alignment of the window will be obtained in exact relation to the square of the mat. Instead of this method, the lines can be ruled with the aid of a square, but the other process is better.

(2) To produce a sharp-edged cut, a fresh strip of cardboard should be placed under the line of every new cut, for otherwise the knife can easily slip and make a jagged edge on the bevel.

(3) To keep the ruler in place and prevent it from slipping, it is a good idea to paste strips of thin sandpaper with rubber cement to the underside of the ruler which will rest on the board.

(4) Draw the knife firmly, holding it at a slant, along the beveled edge of the ruler from one corner of the marked window to the other. Never change the angle of the cut while making it or the bevel will appear wavy. After the cut has been made, the center board will usually adhere to the corners of the window. To detach the board completely, use a razor blade, carefully *holding it flush with the bevel* and loosen the board so it falls out and leaves your window clear.

The thicker the board, the more difficult it will be to produce an even bevel, for it takes a lot of pressure to cut through the tough paper fiber. In fact, cutting the paper dulls the knife more quickly even than cutting wood, therefore it is necessary to resharpen the knife on a flat sharpening stone moistened liberally with machine oil after cutting *each one* of the window sides.

As for the windows, generally speaking, they should be made wide enough to come exactly to the edges of the picture being framed, unless some outer part of a print is desired to be covered. For etchings (and some prints, when desired) the opening should be wide enough to go ⅛″ to ¼″ beyond the edge of the plate—on the top and the sides—and as much below as is needed to leave the signature or any other inscriptions visible.

To determine the window area of any picture it is a good idea to lay loose paper along the four edges and move them in and out to see exactly at which points you wish the mat to come, then mark faintly with a pencil the established points for the window. This is especially advisable on drawings and lithographs where the outer edges are seldom established as clearly as they are, for instance, on an etching or any printed engraving.

CUTTING GLASS

After the frame and the insert or mat have been made, and the picture has been attached to a mount, cut the glass.

The only instruments needed for this process are a good steel ruler and a glass cutter. Diamond points are the best cutters but they are quite expensive. The ordinary kind obtainable in hardware stores, however, will generally serve the purpose well.

Cutting glass is a relatively easy procedure and anyone can acquire the requisite skill with a little practice. The requirements for a successful job are few but they must be observed with meticulous care.

(1) The glass should be placed on a cardboard-covered work bench. The surface *must* be perfectly even and flat.

(2) The glass must be perfectly clean so as to allow the cutter to glide over it with even pressure. The best way to clean the glass is with alcohol mixed with chalk powder or with one of the commercial solutions for window cleaning. A piece of scrunched up newspaper cleans off either solution beautifully.

(3) Since the shaft of the cutter will exert a pressure against the ruler, immobilize the ruler so that it will not slide on the slick glass surface. This can be done by inserting nails into the bench on one side (away from the pressure) and outside the glass surface. A piece of adhesive tape (made from paper or linen) can also be attached to the reverse side of the ruler to prevent it from slipping.

(4) Start at the far end and draw the glass cutter toward you with a firm and constant pressure in one straight line, holding the cutter at a moderate slant toward you. One should never go over a cut a second time, and do not start your cut by going over the sharp glass edge, for this will dull the cutter. Should the first attempt at effecting a straight cut be unsuccessful, the glass should be discarded or it should be cut to a smaller size. Better to try your skill on a few pieces of broken or discarded glass before attempting to cut the piece for your frame.

To cut the glass plate after the scoring has been made, tap it gently *on the reverse side* at both ends of the cut, and part the glass by bending it slightly *downward from the cut.* Never tap the glass in the middle of the cut and do not apply undue pressure when trying to part it.

9

MITER CUTTING AND JOINING (for assembling frames and inserts)

Cutting and joining the mitered ends of a molding are not difficult either but they require considerable accuracy. With a little practice on odd pieces of wood the beginner or occasional frame maker should acquire the necessary familiarity with his tools to do a good precision job.

The following is a list of tools and supplies needed for making or putting a frame together:

1. A good substantial miter box and saw.

2. A Stanley Marsh miter vise. This tool is designed expressly for joining frames. It clamps both the pieces of molding together while the joint is glued or nailed. If you do not have a miter vise available, an ordinary bench vise will do.

3. A stop block for the miter box. This device enables one easily to cut mitered pieces of the same length. Attach a yardstick to the back of the fence of the miter box. On the opposite end from the saw blade is an adjustable block of wood, fastened to the yardstick with a small C clamp (see diagram XXIV).

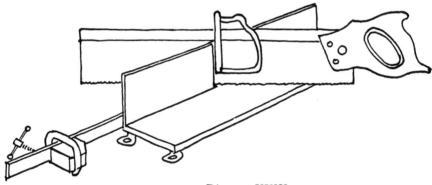

Diagram XXIV.

4. Weldwood (a synthetic glue) or carpenters' hide glue.
5. Thin finishing nails of various lengths.
6. Hammer.
7. Drill.
8. Nail set.
9. Crack filler (plastic wood).

To join the frame properly, you must give the following factors careful attention:

a. Both mitered ends of each of the four pieces of molding must be an exact 45° angle. Be sure the saw is vertical to the molding when making these cuts.

b. The two end pieces must be exactly the same length, and the two side pieces must be exactly the same length for the assembled frame to form a true square or rectangle.

c. The joining must be flush and smooth with no protruding points which would leave undesirable cracks or holes when the pieces are assembled.

Before mitering, the long piece of molding is cut straight across into four lengths. This will allow for more convenient handling. In cutting these lengths be sure to allow twice the width of the molding plus 3 inches extra for the insert (provided this is being used). As an example, let's assume we have a 16″ x 20″ picture and that the molding is 3″ wide. The longer lengths would measure 29″, (20″ plus 6″ plus 3″) and the shorter ones 25″ (16″ plus 6″ plus 3″) (see diagram XXV).

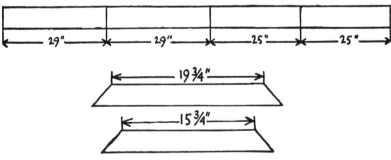

Diagram XXV.

We now proceed to miter the ends. Set the miter box saw gauge at a 45° angle and saw the left ends of all four pieces. Make sure that the miter box is either permanently attached to the work bench or is securely clamped down—the piece of molding being cut should be face up, with the inside, or rabbet edge, held firmly against the fence to prevent any shifting while making the cut. Be sure to have the rabbet edge away from you when sawing or the corner will be rough.

After the four pieces have been mitered on the left end, swing the saw gauge around to the opposite 45° angle. Before mitering the right ends, the following simple formula must be observed to determine the exact measurement for the cuts—using the 16″ x 20″ picture size and a molding with a ¼″ rabbet as an example. Along the extreme inside edge of the frame, which is the lip of the rabbet, measure from the already-mitered end 15¾″ and mark with a pencil. This is the point where the right miter cut will begin for the short piece, 19¾″ for the long piece. These figures are arrived at thus: 16″ (picture dimension) plus ¼″ (tolerance) minus ½″ (twice the depth of the rabbet) equals 15¾″ for short piece. 20″ plus ¼″ minus ½″ equals 19¾″ for the long piece. Now cut the right ends at the correct markings on the two pieces. To make the duplicates of these pieces, use the stop block, clamped in position on the stick, at a point determined by the length of the finished piece (see diagram XXVI).

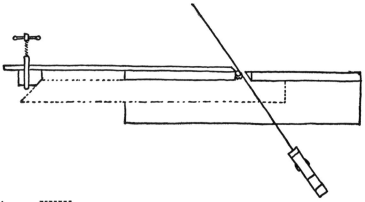

Diagram XXVI.

Now we proceed to join the four pieces with glue and finishing nails. This operation gives many beginners trouble. The secret lies in the fact that all nail holes must be drilled first. With a long and a short piece held firmly in position in the miter vise, drill a hole entirely through the first piece and just a little into the second piece. Remove the first piece from the vise and apply glue. Replace glued piece in vise and tighten both pieces in perfect position. Now drive nails almost all the way in. Next, reverse the nailing procedure and drill and nail from the opposite side, making sure to aim the holes so that the crossed nails do not hit each other. Then countersink nails with a nail set. Join the other set of short and long pieces. Remove any glue that may have been squeezed out of the joint with a rag. Glue is very troublesome if it is allowed to harden. When joining the first two pieces with the second two pieces to complete the frame, it is necessary to place a support under the end that is not in the vise. If this precaution is not observed, the unsupported joint might open up because of the undue strain. If you do not have a miter vise, you can use an ordinary bench vise. Place one piece of molding in the vise horizontally and hold the other piece with your hand. You will have to use a try square to square the corner.

Two sizes of nails are usually required for joining, the longer one for the inside, the shorter outside. Fill all countersunk nail holes with crack filler (plastic wood) and sandpaper when dry. Try to have the joint as smooth and nearly flush as possible. If there is a slight discrepancy, let it be on the back of the molding rather than on the face. *For frames with inserts*—the insert is made first with the same precision and procedure as described above. The frame is then made to fit the insert.

10

FRAMING OF COLOR REPRODUCTIONS *(and general notes on framing)*

The importance of a frame that is in good style and is appropriate for oil paintings, on the one hand, and water colors and drawings, on the other, has already been dealt with in this book, and many specific finishes have been given. It has also been emphasized that a poorly chosen or indifferent looking frame will reduce the general decorative effect of a painting.

In this section frames for reproductions of oil paintings (that is, color reproductions on paper) are featured. The study of these will further demonstrate the wide variety of frame finishes that are possible. Any of these styles or finishes can be adapted for use on water colors, drawings, and original oil paintings, provided the reader takes into account the different mechanical requirements, such as the width of the molding, the use of glass and a mat for graphic work, the use of the insert in oil painting, and the like, all of which have been dealt with previously. These illustrations will also further demonstrate suitable proportions between the size of the picture, the insert or the mat, and the frame.

When we consider the framing of color reproductions, the appearance of the frame is of even greater importance than for an original work of art, for without a spectacular frame—one of high decorative appeal—a reproduction, no matter how faithful and true to the original, will always look cheap.

In contrast to frames for most oil paintings—which frames in general retain a rather conservative character—frames for color reproductions are most effective when they are somewhat novel in design. Just how far to go in the direction of originality is a question of individual taste, and the decorator may always be at variance with the artist on this score—about any frame, for that matter, whether designed for an original oil, a water color,

Fig. 37. Color reproduction by a XVth century Florentine master. *A
deep molding curves gently toward the picture. The beveled inside
section, which takes the place of an insert, is finished in gold leaf and
the design of scrolls was drawn on the combed gesso before it hardened.
A warm gray patina was brushed over the curved molding before it
received a polished wax finish. (Courtesy F. A. R. Gallery, New York.)*

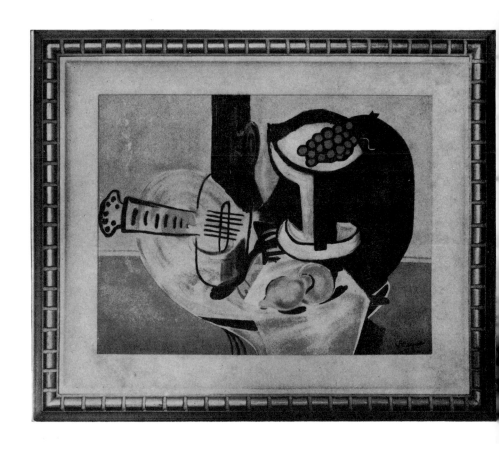

Fig. 38. Color reproduction by Georges Braque. *The inside scoop mold-*
ing is 2″ deep and 3″ wide. It is covered with a white gesso textured
with an extra-fine comb (see finishes 12, 13 in chapter IV) to break up
an otherwise completely flat finish. The outside profile is carved and
gilded. The heavy geometric design on the profile goes well with the
bold forms in the reproduction. (Courtesy Lewensohn Co., Inc., New
York.)

Fig. 39. Color reproduction, detail from a fresco by Michelangelo. *This print was mounted on a ¾″-thick panel and placed in a frame known as a "shadow box." The background of the frame is finished in finely textured gesso of terra cotta color. To make a "shadow box" frame, use an unrabbeted piece of molding and miter it on edge rather than flat as on the lid of a wooden box. The background can be glued and nailed to the molding. (Courtesy F. A. R. Gallery, New York.)*

Fig. 40. Color reproduction by Chirico. *This painting has an extra-wide frame made up of three separate moldings. The flat center piece is combed in heavy gesso, revealing a dark ground underneath. Simple lines are employed in the design of the profile, and the tones of the frame are harmonized with the grays and browns of the picture. (Courtesy F. A. R. Gallery, New York.)*

Fig. 41. Colored reproduction by Renoir. *A wide panel frame with a high-back molding set close to the picture. The tones of the frame are predominantly in grays to set off the rich colors of the painting. The textured effect on the wide panel was done by scratching with a comb in a crisscross fashion into the wet gray gesso finish, revealing the white gesso undercoat. (Courtesy F. A. R. Gallery, New York.)*

Fig. 42. An etching by Jean Louis Forain *set in a ⅜″ thick mat covered in silk and with a white bevel. The frame is a facsimile of a style current during the reign of Louis XVI. (Courtesy F. A. R. Gallery, New York.)*

Fig. 43. Color reproduction of a Japanese print. *The outside profile has a multi-colored finish (on top of white gesso). The cardboard mat is of green color applied over a pebbled gesso surface. The bevel of the mat carries an antiqued silver leaf over a red priming (see chapter VII). (Courtesy Lewensohn Co., Inc., New York.)*

Fig. 44. Reproduction, detail from a fresco by Piero della Francesca. *This lovely detail of a fresco is shown in a variation of the panel frame. An insert with black velvet pasted over it encloses the picture; the adjoining flat profile is in highly burnished gold leaf. The outside frame is in combed gesso painted dull black. All these processes are described earlier in the book. (Courtesy F. A. R. Gallery, New York.)*

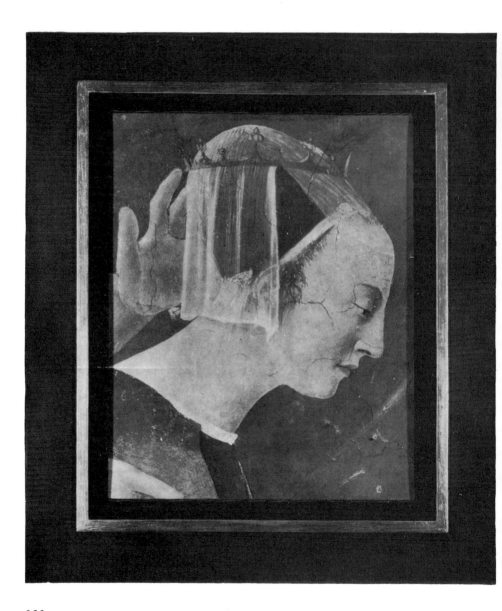

Fig. 45. Silk screen on Canson paper by Umberto Romano (Associated American Artists Galleries). *The inner and outer moldings are finished in gold leaf (see chapter VII) and the insert in gray gesso. The flat center molding is covered with a coarse linen, which is glued to the wood and primed with red color (venetian red bound by glue size). On top of this color, a cerulean blue glue-color paint (chapter II) has been applied thinly to permit the red to come through. (Courtesy Lewensohn Co., Inc., New York.)*

Fig. 46. Color reproduction by M. Utrillo. *The architectural motifs of the picture are enhanced here by the wide comb marks in a light brownish gesso. The deep marks of the comb reveal the dark underlying color. The inset is painted a light color to match the tone of the light areas of the main moldings. (Courtesy F. A. R. Gallery, New York.)*

Fig. 47 (opposite page). Color reproduction by Picasso. *The simple wide frame is made up from a white insert 1" wide, and a scoop molding (3½") which is finished in gray gesso and rubbed through so as to bring out the grain of the wood. (Courtesy Lewensohn Co., Inc., New York.)*

Fig. 49. Color reproduction by Georges Braque. *In this frame of a most simple design, emphasis was given to the finish of the flat panel, which is covered with silver leaf. The silver surface was treated with sulphur to produce mottled effects (see chapter VII under "Glazing and tarnishing metal-leaf surfaces"). Some of the dark priming underneath comes through, giving to the whole a rather rich antique appearance. (Courtesy F. A. R. Gallery, New York.)*

Fig. 48 (opposite page). Color reproduction by Marc Chagall. *Here a white edging to the print is allowed to show in the frame, displaying the artist's signature. This white area sets off the inside profile of the frame, which is finished in antiqued gold (see chapter VII). The wide center section has a pebbled gesso surface painted in a flat black casein color, and the outside molding is made of oak. This molding has been scorched to a dark color and some blue pigment was rubbed into its surface for an interesting texture. (Courtesy Lewensohn Co., Inc., New York.)*

Fig. 50. A color lithograph by Georges Rouault. *The gilded frame is a copy of an early 18th-century Spanish pattern. (Courtesy F. A. R. Gallery, New York.)*

Fig. 51 (opposite page). Color reproduction by Georges Rouault. *A heavy, wide frame has been used to complement the powerfully designed picture. The inner flat surface is finished in gold leaf on red ground, well rubbed and scratched for an antique look, and the outer receding section is in textured gesso, toned to correspond to the darker colors of the painting. (Courtesy F. A. R. Gallery, New York.)*

139

Fig. 52. A color etching by Georges Braque, one of the illustrations from *L'ordre des oiseaux* of St.-John Perse. *The unusual tubular frame is polished brass.* (*Courtesy F. A. R. Gallery, New York.*)

or a reproduction. The decorator will have in mind the total effect of the framed picture in relation to the decoration of the room, whereas a painter will look at it from the point of view of the painting alone, and will tend to be more conservative in his taste. The painter's point of view may well be influenced by the fact that the paint technique is an ancient craft, hence it is inexorably bound to the past and its traditions. The medium of color reproduction, on the other hand, is thoroughly modern; it has no traditional ties and therefore need not be guided by a spirit such as may influence the framing of originals.

In the preceding pages, the illustrations demonstrate how reproduction prints can be effectively framed. It should be noted that these and all such reproductions should be solidly mounted on thick fiber board as described in chapter VIII and should be further protected by a coat of plastic varnish or shellac unless they are to be framed behind glass. Without such a protection dust will work into the paper and gradually ruin the reproduction.

11

THE HANGING OF PICTURES

Quite often pictures are hung too high on the wall. Paintings of small size (up to 20″ x 24″, for example) should be centered at about eye level. Larger paintings, because they must be viewed from a distance, should be hung a little higher, but no picture should be placed so high on the wall as to make close inspection difficult.

It is best to hang oil paintings so that they will be lighted from a side window, for if the light comes from the front, the surface gloss will make parts of the painting invisible. The only way to remedy the latter condition is to tilt the upper part of the painting slightly from the wall and toward the source of light. This can be done by wedging a small piece of block behind the upper part of the picture. The block will be held by the pressure of the frame against the wall. Another way is to place the screw eyes lower than you normally would on the back of the frame so the picture tilts forward. The desire of many people for a flat surface appearance in a painting, a surface which will not reflect light, is unreasonable. All paintings must be protected by varnish which will always make a painting glossy. The so-called mat varnishes have proved ineffectual. Moreover, to show the proper value and depth of colors, a paint surface must always be glossy. The same applies to color reproductions which receive a coat of plastic varnish or shellac, or water colors and drawings behind glass, which will also reflect the light.

If the daylight does not afford a proper lighting for a painting, the use of artificial light will be needed. Direct lighting such as provided by the conventional reflector attached to the upper part of a frame is not an ideal solution, and is somewhat obsolete in style. Special lighting from a hidden light fixture which illuminates one picture only is fine if you can afford it. Such fixtures can be installed only by a specialist, however, and are therefore quite expensive. Short of such special indirect lighting fixtures, you will have to effect the best compromise possible.

As to the actual hanging of a picture, the customary way of hammering a single nail or hook in the wall is not the best, for the picture will easily slide to a crooked position on its wire. The approved way is to hammer two picture hooks at the height desired and a little less than the width of the picture apart. The hanging wire, when placed over these hooks will hold the picture firmly in place with little slippage. A wise precaution before nailing the hooks into a plaster wall is to place a piece of Scotch tape over the place marked for the hook. Then when you hammer the nail into the wall, the plaster will hold firm and not widen into a large hole.

Picture-frame wire, obtainable at hardware stores, is the most-used support for pictures, although heavy string or a light cord is also acceptable. As a matter of fact, some people prefer the latter as it is less likely to slip on the hooks than will wire. Use a piece of cord about five times the width of the picture frame. Run the cord through each eye, double thickness, so that it extends through about the same length at each end. Then bring each double end back through the same eye but from the opposite direction. Tie the double ends together, leaving some slack. Pull out the loops around the eyes so that they are equal in length, and fasten these loops to the hooks on the wall. These individual loops hold the picture fast without any possibility of its slipping once it is in place. You must be careful to get the wall hooks exactly parallel, otherwise of course the picture will be slanted.

Whether you plan to use picture wire or cord, fasten screw eyes into the two side pieces at the back of the frame, just above center. Bore a hole first with a gimlet before attempting to insert the screws. If you are using picture wire, insert a single or double length of wire, according to whether it is a light or heavy frame, through the eyes of the screws, and bend the ends of the wire back over the screws, winding it around the hanging cross piece until both loose ends are used up.

SOURCES OF MATERIALS AND FRAMES

Consult the Yellow Pages of the telephone directory of your nearest town or city for artist-material stores, picture framing shops, lumber yards and mills, paint stores, etc. If they do not have the items you need in stock, they can probably order them for you. The following dealers regularly carry the items listed:

Custom-made moldings: lumber mills.

Builders' moldings: lumber yards.

Raw-wood moldings, frames, and all artists' materials: A. C. Friedrichs Co., 140 Sullivan Street, New York 10012; Arthur Brown & Bros., Inc., 2 W. 46 St., New York 10036.

Decorative bead moldings and machine-carved moldings: Bendix Mfg. Co., 192 Lexington Ave., New York 10016.

Custom-made frames and stock frames: Leo Robinson, 1388 Sixth Ave., New York 10019; F.A.R. Gallery, 746 Madison Ave., New York 10021.

Gold, metal, silver leaf, gilders' clay, whiting, dry pigments, rottenstone, glue, gelatin, japan size, dragon's blood, gamboge, shellac, carnauba wax, beeswax: H. Behlen & Bros., 10 Christopher St., New York 10014.

Dry pigments: Fezandie & Sperrle, Inc., 103 Lafayette St., New York 10007.

Stanley Marsh picture frame vise: hardware stores; Stanley Tools, New Britain, Conn.